BERLIN UNDERGROUND

AN INTERNATIONAL DETECTIVE THRILLER

LUKE RICHARDSON

1

Epitome Nightclub, Berlin. Present Day.

MINTY ROLLESTON GRIPPED his bottle of beer, his knuckles turning white, as he saw two men pace towards him across the nightclub dance floor. The techno beat from the state-of-the-art sound system dwindled into silence as his heart raced. The men locked their gaze on Minty. Something in those icy stares told Minty everything he needed to know; the men were here to kill him.

Minty backed away through the dance floor, pushing past a group of people stomping to the bass-heavy beat. He swung left and ran between a dozen people, all dancing in a line, facing up towards the DJ, who seamlessly mixed in the next record. Minty reached the back of the club and spun around. Any light from the overhead strobes which made it to the back of the club was lost amid the thick black drapes and black paint. Minty stood in the dimly lit space and stared back onto the dance floor.

The brutish men barged in Minty's direction, sending dancers stumbling left and right. Although Minty's quick movement had bought him time, the men were still close behind.

Turning on his heels, Minty dashed across the club, staying in the shadows as much as he could. With fewer dancers here, the going was quick. As Minty ran, thoughts spun through his mind. Someone had set him up, that he knew for sure. But who that person was, he had no idea.

Without turning around, Minty darted from the room and out into the narrow corridor which ran between the nightclub's various rooms. Two different techno beats clashed, vibrating the bricks of the old power station-turned-nightclub. Minty had spent many years stomping around this nightclub's various dance floors, enjoying the performances of DJs and music producers from all over the world.

A thought flitted through Minty's consciousness: the nightclub was a fitting place to end his time in Berlin. This place was one reason he came here to begin with. It occurred to Minty that the man who he was supposed to be meeting here had done that on purpose.

"Kaspar, where are you?" Minty hissed between clenched teeth.

Footsteps thumped across the floor behind him, almost, but not completely, obscured by the music. Minty spun around a moment too late. The thugs charged up behind him, mere feet away. Somehow, they had made up time crossing the dance floor. In the meagre light from distant bulkhead lights, Minty saw the men clearly for the first time. All muscles and bones. These guys wore malice as though it were a fashion accessory.

Minty recognized one man. He drew a panicked lungful of air. The head of Berlin's most ruthless underworld operation, Olezka Ivankov was not a man you wanted to mess with. That Olezka had come to deal with this himself was also not good news. The Russian Kingpin clearly had a score to settle and wanted to see it done personally.

Fortunately, the men had dropped into single file in the narrow passage. Olezka took the rear, while his associate was in the lead. That was good news for Minty, as only the leading man could strike. That's exactly what he did. The leading man slowed and swung an arm the size of a battering ram towards Minty's throat. Minty saw the arm coming, muscles standing out like hydraulic pistons. For the briefest time, everything seemed to move in slow motion as Minty considered his options. Minty thought about ducking and running, but the man was too close. Even if Minty could get out of the way of this strike, there would be more, many, many more.

Minty glanced down at the half-full bottle of beer in his hand. He hadn't put the thing down. Minty lurched forward and swung the bottle through the air. He smashed the bottle into the side of the leading man's head. The bottle shattered, tearing into the skin on the side of the man's shaved scalp. The brute's expression melted from one of calculated rage, to confusion, and finally on to pain. A mixture of warm beer and blood spewed down the brute's face, neck and into his shirt.

With both hands, Minty shoved the man backward. Although it felt as though he were pushing against a brick wall, the man was disorientated and retreated a step, colliding with Olezka.

Olezka shouted, his voice as guttural as a ship's horn, and tried to surge forward and grab Minty. Not realizing his subordinate's injury, Olezka smashed into the other man. Both men stumbled together, groaning. Olezka almost lost his footing but supported himself on the wall at the last minute.

Blood and beer splashed against the cold concrete floor from the leading man's face.

Certain that the blows would delay his pursuers, Minty spun around and sprinted on. Several violent words in a language Minty didn't speak cut through the monstrous bassline of one of Luuka Syence's latest tracks. At the end of the corridor, Minty glanced behind him, saw the thugs struggle back to their feet and rush on.

Minty had increased his lead but not for long. His feet almost slipping, he sprinted into the bar area. Smoke and anticipation hung in the air as people queued for drinks, nodding to the infectious beat.

His eyes darting from left to right, Minty searched for a way out. Despite his frantic appearance, no one paid him any attention — they were used to all sorts of people in places like this. Suddenly, he spied a familiar face in the crowd. A pair of blue-gray eyes locked onto his.

"Kaspar," Minty groaned, racing across the room. The slender German whom Minty had got to know over the last few months stood at the far side of the room. Kaspar's demeanor was as natural as though he was waiting for a drink.

"I'm afraid we're in some trouble," the German said in accented English. "Someone has let... how you say... the cat from the bag."

Minty tried to stutter a reply, but suddenly found that he was too out of breath.

"Follow me," Kaspar said, striding towards the rear corner of the room.

Minty followed, unquestioning.

Reaching the wall, Kaspar pulled aside one of the black

drapes and slipped through. Minty ducked under and found that they were in a narrow passageway which ran further into the building. Minty imagined that the old power station, built during the Soviet era, was a warren of such passageways.

Minty closely followed Kaspar through the shadows. Somewhere beyond the walls, the techno-beat from the nightclub's dance floors continued to grunt and groan.

Kaspar paused at the end of the passageway and pulled aside another drape. The Russian peered out into the nightclub. Minty saw bright beams of light sweeping above black-clad dancers. They had made their way back to the main dance floor. The space was a pulsating sea of bodies, moving in harmonious chaos to the music's rhythm.

"We've bought some time," Kaspar said, his voice roughened by years of smoking strong tobacco. "Now, to get out of here."

Kaspar paused before slipping out onto the dance floor. Minty followed, momentarily dazed by the lights which strobed and flickered. Minty glanced around, searching for their pursuers. Shapes moved in the shadows at the edge of the dance floor. Minty had no way of knowing whether the movement was innocent dancers or the thugs who were now no-doubt baying for his blood.

Kaspar pushed between the lines of dancers and Minty hurried to follow. Minty glanced at the people as he passed, all of them lost in the music. The club and the beat felt so alien now. He turned sideways and slipped between the dancers' gyrating bodies, all slick with sweat.

In the past, that had been him — getting lost in the music. But now he just wanted out.

Casting a brief glance back at the space behind the drape, Minty hoped that their pursuers were unaware of this secret thoroughfare. When Minty spun back around, Kaspar was a few steps ahead, and cutting quickly through the crowd. Minty hurried to keep up.

Minty and Kaspar had met several times. The German was the man who had visited Minty in the shop to exchange the packages for the cash.

Minty knew little about the packages, except that they originated in South America, and were often sent along with the fabrics he used to make his clothes.

There was something dodgy going on, of that Minty was certain, but didn't care. The bags of money had kept Minty's business afloat for many years and allowed him to enjoy the finer side of Berlin.

Truth be told, Minty had liked Kaspar from the start. Unlike most of the men, Kaspar didn't seem like just another thug. There was intelligence in Kaspar's cold, gray eyes.

Kaspar picked up his pace, turning into the nightclub's central staircase. He took the stairs quickly, people darting out of his way. Minty noticed that people moved aside as the German approached. It wasn't that the man looked tough, but there was something about him, a glimmer in his eyes that exuded a warning.

At the bottom of the stairs, Minty heard the noise — a raised voice, followed by the pounding of heavy footsteps on the stairs above. He spun around and saw the thugs charging down the staircase. The thugs shoved their way through a group of partygoers climbing the other way, sending two young men falling to their knees.

Minty stood, dazed by the sight. The thugs barreled closer. The face of the leading man was covered with blood, making him look even more ghoulish than usual. That guy was really going to enjoy causing Minty some pain.

Kaspar dragged Minty away, shaking him back into action. The pair shoved out through a fire escape. Once outside, they sprinted around a line of people which snaked around the corner — in Berlin; the night was still young.

Minty glanced over his shoulder, catching sight of their pursuers bursting out through the door.

2

Minty and Kaspar darted down a quiet street, determined to put as much distance between themselves and their pursuers as possible. Minty glanced behind him as they turned a corner. Olezka and his assistant were still on their tail. Although these men were brutes, they didn't seem to move as quickly as Minty and Kaspar could. That, at least, was an advantage.

Minty and Kaspar careened around a tight corner, feet skidding on wet cobblestones, their hearts hammering in their chests.

Kaspar gestured urgently towards a narrow alleyway up ahead. Without hesitation, they darted into the passage, skirting a parked car which looked like it had been there for months, jumping over a pile of broken glass.

Minty glanced over his shoulder. Although their pursuers were now cloaked by the shadows, he still heard the distant thudding of boots on the cobbles somewhere back there.

Kaspar reached the end of the passageway first and burst out on to a main road, startling two people ambling toward the nightclub. Kaspar crossed the road, leaped over a dumpster, and disappeared down another passageway. Minty followed a moment later, his heart thudding as though it might break free from his chest altogether.

The pair charged down the passageway, both focused on the light ahead. A minute later, the pair emerged on a wide street, both gasping and out of breath.

Minty glanced at a tram as it rumbled past. The vehicle was full of people either returning home from the night out, or up early for work. It was that time, when both ends of the day seemed to combine for a few nebulous minutes.

Minty and Kaspar charged across the street and jumped a fence into a park. Although Minty was only a few feet behind, he suddenly felt as if Kaspar had been swallowed by the gloom. Minty staggered on until his eyes adjusted and saw moonlight filtering through the branches of gnarled trees, casting eerie silhouettes on the ground. Kaspar ran twenty feet ahead, weaving his way between rusty swings and benches. Minty sprinted off, getting a burst of energy he didn't know he had.

With their pursuers hot on their heels, the duo raced toward a chain-link fence at the far end of the park.

Minty reached the barrier, leaned forward on his knees, and took two deep breaths. He gazed up at the ten-foot-high chain-link. His heart worked its way up his throat and made him want to vomit.

"I can't... I can't get over there," Minty muttered between breaths. He glanced around, looking for another option.

A shout came from somewhere behind, reminding him that their pursuers were closing in every second.

"Sure, you can," Kaspar said, dropping in to a crouch. "It's all about positive attitude, Ja! You think, you do!" Kaspar ran and leaped at the fence. His hands gripped the chain-link like a man-sized squirrel and he pulled himself up. In three heaves, he was at the top. He swung himself over and dropped to the other side.

Minty once again whipped around, looking for another escape route. As the shadowy figures of their pursuers entered the park, he made up his mind for sure.

Minty jumped at the fence, trying to mimic the grace with which Kaspar had climbed. Taller and heavier than Kaspar, the chain-link sagged and twisted under Minty's weight, making the climb even more difficult. Finally, dragging himself hand over hand, Minty made it to the top. He swung himself over, lost his grip and fell, and thumped hard to the ground on the other side. The fall knocked the breath from Minty's lungs and made colors dance in front of his vision.

Kaspar hauled Minty up to his feet. The pair looked out at several railway lines. From where they stood, there appeared to be at least eight pairs of tracks, although Minty couldn't be sure in the gloom. In the distance he locked on the inviting glow of a station.

"That's Warschauer Strasse," Kaspar said, pointing towards the station. "We get there and we're clear."

"I'm not sure. Running across the tracks isn't that..." The distant clatter of an approaching train drowned out Minty's disagreements.

"It'll be fine," Kaspar shouted. "Don't touch the rails and watch out for trains." Kaspar set off at a sprint across the tracks. He hopped over the first rail and scurried across the tie before jumping over the other rail.

From deep within the gloom, the noise of the approaching thugs removed any hope of going back.

Minty shook his head, not quite believing what was happening, and followed the German. "Which one did he say not to touch?" Minty hissed, looking down at the rails. "Don't touch any." He decided, setting off as quickly as he could while avoiding the obstacles.

Minty caught up with Kaspar as they crossed the fourth track. Kaspar had removed his ancient mobile phone from his pocket and was poking at the buttons. "Phone's not working. Battery must be dead," Kaspar said.

"Maybe it's time for an upgrade," Minty said, stepping off the track and standing beside Kaspar. "How did they find out, anyway?" His voice sounded like the noise of a deflating tire.

"No idea." Kaspar shrugged, stuffing his phone in the pocket of his long green coat. "Olezka must have worked it out. It doesn't matter now. We are almost home and free."

"But what about me?" Minty said, panic lacing his voice. "I need to get out of here. What about my money?"

Kaspar turned his ice-cold stare on Minty. "I have that all under control. We continue as normal. I will get you your money in the next forty-eight hours."

Minty wanted to argue, but somehow the German's stare forced him into silence.

Minty broke the stare, glancing up at the sky. Spikes of bruised purple scudded across the heavens. Minty's eyes were drawn to a pair of small birds skipping between the buildings. They darted this way and that, their twittering song sharp and shrill in the still morning air. The city was coming alive one wingbeat at a time.

Thirty feet away, a freight train slipped through the shadows. The ground shook beneath Minty's feet.

"Let's go," Kaspar said, pointing towards the train. "We use that as cover. They won't see where we're going." Kaspar sprinted towards the rear of the freight train and rounded the last railcar, disappearing from sight. Minty followed as a great melancholy bellow sounded from the train's whistle.

Minty and Kaspar slowed to keep pace with the hulking train, which only proceeded at a walking pace. They peered around the rear car and saw Olezka and his thug climbing over the chain-link fence. Much larger than Minty and Kaspar, the pair found it difficult as the chain-link sagged and curled under their weight. Still, they made the climb and were across within twenty seconds.

"Keep moving," Kaspar hissed, picking up pace towards the station.

Kaspar and Minty ran alongside the freight train and into the station. The station was a hive of activity, even at this early hour. Commuters rushed in all directions, oblivious to the two men sprinting along the tracks.

Kaspar charged across the final set of tracks and scrambled up on to the platform. A woman clearly dressed for work looked at him with a confused expression. She shrugged and turned her attention straight back to her phone.

Minty reached the platform and pulled himself off the tracks. Even though he was taller than the German, he had to heave his way up on to the platform. Minty fought to stand up and took a deep breath of air filled with the smell of diesel.

"Where now?" Minty said, standing beside Kaspar.

"I need to use your phone," Kaspar said, holding his hand out in Minty's direction. "I'll call my driver."

"Use your share of the money to get you a new one," Minty said, fishing his phone from his pocket and passing it across.

"I'm not getting one of those modern ones," Kaspar said, dialing a number from memory. "It's like wearing a tracker around your neck. With this, you're nothing but a pawn in a game." Kaspar turned away and shouted into the phone. Minty heard the distant whine and hiss of a commuter train echoing from another platform. Minty recognized the sound as something quintessential to Berlin's bustling subway system.

"Here you are," Kaspar said, spinning around and thrusting his phone at Minty. "Driver will be here in one minute."

Minty took the phone and Kaspar set off sprinting for the exit, ducking and diving between groups of people.

Minty's eyes darted around the dimly lit platform, taking in the late-night tableau of urban life. A group of disheveled young people, their energy waning after a night out, slouched on a bench. A man with a tangle of dreadlocks nodded rhythmically to music on oversized headphones. In the distance, a train rumbled like a distant nightmare. Its presence felt rather than seen, as if it belonged to the dreams in another sleeper's head.

Distracted, Minty went to slide the phone inside his pocket. The phone slipped from his grasp and fell. Minty turned, watching the device spin down in slow motion. He swung his hand, trying to catch the phone. His fingers clawed through the air, hitting nothing. The device fell and collided with the platform. The screen spider webbed, and the phone bounced up again. Minty crouched, trying once more to grab the device. Again, his hands swept through the air. The phone fell down on to the tracks.

Minty spun around and saw the two thugs charging his way. He glanced at Kaspar, who was already halfway up the stairs.

Kaspar stopped and spun around. "Come on!" He shouted, beckoning madly.

With one more glance down at his phone on the tracks, Minty swung around and charged up the stairs.

"What kept you?" Kaspar said, as Minty reached the top of the stairs and ran through the station concourse.

"I dropped my phone," Minty said, panting. "On the tracks."

"You're better without it," Kaspar said, throwing Minty a grin. "Now, no one will know where you are." Kaspar charged from the station and hopped across the barrier into the road.

A black Mercedes Benz G Class zoomed down the street and screeched to a halt next to them.

Kaspar quickly swung open the passenger door and leaped inside. "Hurry up and get in," he urged.

Minty jumped in the back and the driver floored the gas. As the Mercedes roared away, Minty glanced back at the tracks spanning out below them. The freight train crawled away, issuing another bellow on its horn.

3

Gatwick Airport, London. One week later.

"Oi! Wake up!"

Leo forced his eyes open. It felt as though each one contained a handful of sand. He blinked hard and shook his head. The light stung.

"We're here," Allissa said from her seat across the aisle. "You slept through the entire landing. We all had to listen to your snoring."

Leo rubbed his face. "What? We're what..."

"Yeah, it was funny, especially the bit when you started talking in your sleep. I've got so many questions about..."

"Where are we?" Leo mumbled, not giving in to Allissa's teasing.

"We have landed at London Gatwick Airport." Allissa mimicked the pilot's plummy voice. "And the local time is—"

"Alright, alright. I get it."

"And the outside temperature is... bloody freezing. And I think it's raining."

The plane rolled to a stop, and everyone immediately scrambled to their feet as though it was a race to the door. Leo watched one man scramble to get his bag from the overhead bins as though it was a life or death situation.

Leo sighed and pushed his shoulder blades together. The man in the seat beside him started getting ready to move.

"Just stay still," Leo groaned. "They've not even opened the door. It'll be ages."

Allissa gave Leo a look that he perceived as *appreciative*, although he couldn't be sure. Leo blinked again, trying to remove the colors that danced across his vision. This was typical. After staying awake for the first seven and a half hours of the flight, twisting, and turning with every movement and sound, he eventually dozed off right before landing.

At least it wasn't as bad as their flight from Hong Kong to Abu Dhabi. On that flight, three days earlier, he had just managed to sleep when the person next to him had a need to use the bathroom. Instead of shaking Leo awake with an apology, the man scrambled over him. Although Leo knew this came from a place of courtesy, it didn't mitigate the confusion of waking to find yourself straddled by a stranger.

After a fifteen-minute wait, the air-bridge was connected, and people shuffled forward. Leo waited another two minutes, and only when the aisle was clear, unfolded himself from the seat.

"It's not fair," Leo said, pulling his bag down from the overhead compartment and finally ambling towards the exit.

"What?"

"You close your eyes before we've even taken off and sleep the whole way," Leo moaned. "Why can't I do that?"

"Probably because you're too busy moaning," Allissa quipped.

"That's not true. I never... well, rarely moan."

"At least now we're going home, and you can have a proper sleep like a happy baby," Allissa said, in an annoying voice.

An hour later, Leo and Allissa pushed through the crowds toward the train station. Leo squinted, trying to keep himself awake, while Allissa walked bright-eyed and rejuvenated, beside him.

Although the case in Hong Kong had been trying for them both, Leo had found it emotionally draining. More through luck than design, he'd finally caught up with the woman who'd forced him into the world of missing people to begin with.

Leo had spent over two years looking for Mya. Throughout that time, though, he'd never considered what he would do if he actually found her. Talk to her, he supposed, try to understand why she left. In reality, however, he had no idea what to say or do. The meeting felt to Leo like an oil-covered beach or a desiccated forest. Mya had once been something beautiful and pure, but not anymore.

For the last three days, Leo and Allissa had been staying in a five-star hotel in Abu Dhabi. Since they had to stop there anyway, Allissa suggested they make the most of it. They'd spent the time in their twin beds watching American comedies on the giant TV, visiting the resort's spa and pools, and eating in the lavish restaurants. Allissa had found it therapeutic, but to Leo, it had been the opposite.

Unable to sleep on that first night, he understood the reason. Their relationship was simple before Leo had found Mya. They enjoyed spending time together, and they were good at finding missing people. The upshot of which, whether Leo liked it or not, he and Allissa had landed themselves with a business.

It was a business that required them both; Leo knew that. Although they were both resourceful investigators, Allissa was the driving force behind the business. Money, to Leo — providing his credit cards still worked — was an irrelevance. To Allissa, it was a way of life. She seemed to understand what they needed for each job. She discussed sums with clients that made Leo squirm. She made the bookings, allocated funds, and somehow ensured there was enough left over for them to make a profit.

Allissa also had a fierce sense of right and wrong. Where Leo might have been ready to give up on an investigation, Allissa would carry on until all the loose ends were tied. But it wasn't her business acumen or her investigatory prowess that now worried Leo.

Before Leo had caught up with Mya, things between Allissa and himself were simple. He was looking for Mya. But now that door was closed, Leo could do what he wanted. That brought with it a wave of mayhem, misunderstanding and misery. There was no longer anything in the way.

Watching Allissa's eyes flick across the landscape, Leo knew things had changed. An unfamiliar feeling consumed him now, and Leo didn't like it.

"Are you looking forward to seeing Archie and Lucy?" Leo asked when they were in a taxi speeding through Brighton toward their flat. Large coffees imbibed on the train had taken the edge from his exhaustion. Leo could now see straight and almost hold a normal conversation.

"Yes," Allissa said, "though I'm not sure what it'll be like. We've not really spoken for years."

Archie and Lucy were Allissa's older half brother and sister. After learning what their father had done to her mother, Allissa had cut all contact with the family. Reuniting after her father was finally sent to prison, they had all promised to keep in touch. At the time, Allissa had doubted it. So, when she'd received an invitation to Lucy's birthday party, Allissa decided she had to attend.

"Are you sure you'll be alright without me for a day? What're you going to do on your own?" Allissa said, grinning.

"Can't wait," Leo said, still gazing out the window. He watched the city stream past and realized how cold their apartment would be. There would be washing to do and mail to sort — the general business of society from which Leo took no joy.

"It'll be good to tidy the place up," Leo said.

"You sure? You can come?"

"No, thanks." Leo turned to face Allissa. "I'm going to get some sleep and try to catch up on the invoices we've not done for ages. That means we can afford to eat next week."

Allissa tried to suppress a grin. She doubted Leo even knew how to raise an invoice.

The taxi rounded a corner, and the sea flickered into view between the buildings. It looked gray and somber. It was a world away from the azure blue pool they'd been in the day before.

"On the right here," Allissa said as the taxi turned into their street. The large Victorian houses lining the street looked drab and bleak in the gray morning. "Thanks, just here!" Allissa shouted as the taxi driver shot past their house. The driver slammed to a stop and reversed, soliciting several honks from passing cars.

"Honestly." Leo sighed. "It's fine, here will do."

The taxi driver punched a button on the meter and pointed to the price.

Leo eased out his wallet and looked inside.

"Got any cash?" Leo asked.

Allissa shook her head.

"Can I use my card?"

The taxi driver scowled. He apparently disliked the idea of Leo's payment going through the traditional channels as much as he disliked the idea of stopping in the right place. When Leo laid out the alternative of receiving his fare in Hong Kong Dollars, the taxi driver conceded that the card payment was better than that *funny money*.

The car sped off the moment Leo and Allissa were clear of the vehicle.

Above them, a pair of seagulls flashed from one building to another. Noticing their sorrowful shrieking, Leo looked up. To him, that was the sound of home.

4

"Oh great, my dress has arrived," Allissa said, stepping into their flat's communal entrance hall. Before being split into apartments, the top one of which was Leo and Allissa's, the place would have been a grand three-story residence, no doubt occupied by one of the city's wealthier residents. This former grandeur was hinted at by the entrance hall's intricate plaster moldings and patterned floor tiles, which now struggled for attention from behind a veneer of filth.

"I ordered it while we were in Abu Dhabi," Allissa said, holding up the package.

"Did you, I don't remember? I hope it fits," Leo said, following Allissa up the stairs.

Leo dropped their bags in the living room and looked around. The place was a mess, exactly as he remembered. Discolored paint curled from the walls, and the carpet was so threadbare that in places the floorboards were visible. Leo's computer sat on a desk in the bay window amid piles of books and papers.

Leo and Allissa had discussed moving somewhere more luxurious now that the business was profitable, but considering the time they spent here, and how little they honestly cared, neither had done anything about it.

"Yeah, glad it's here," Allissa said, padding into the kitchen and filling the kettle. "I'm going to have a shower and then try it on." Allissa held up the package, turned and headed for her bedroom. "Tell me what you think, alright? Be honest!"

Before Allissa moved in, the second and smaller bedroom had been unused. The rent in the rundown apartment was so cheap that Leo had never even considered having a housemate. He had to admit, though; he enjoyed Allissa being around.

The kettle rumbled to the boil and Leo paced into the kitchen. He grabbed the canister of instant coffee, pulled off the lid, and stuck a spoon inside. Grinning, he remembered Allissa had pranked him two weeks ago by swapping the canisters around. Leo suppressed a giggle and pulled the tea canister from the shelf. There was no way he would acknowledge the change. That would be tantamount to letting Allissa win.

"Coffee's on the table," Leo said, hearing Allissa pad back into the front room. He was lying back on the sofa with his eyes shut, hoping that at some point soon the room would stop spinning after the long journey.

"There's no milk, I'm afraid," Leo continued, still without opening his eyes. "Or rather, there is milk, but it's been there for so long it's developed its own ecosystem. To be fair, you take your life in your hands even by opening the..."

"What do you think?" Allissa interrupted.

"Well, it's pretty gross." Leo pinched the bridge of his nose. Colors danced in his vision. "We should have emptied it before we left..."

"No, what do you think about the dress?"

Leo opened his eyes and sat up. His eyes widened, and his jaw dropped.

Having known each other for almost a year, Leo was used to looking away as Allissa passed him wrapped in a towel or only wearing her underwear. Those moments, however, did nothing to prepare him for what he saw now.

As his eyes ran across her body, Leo couldn't help but feel a rush of emotion. The black dress adorned her like a masterpiece, accentuating every curve and contour. It clung to her in all the right places, highlighting her natural grace and elegance.

"What? You don't like it?" Allissa asked, turning around gracefully, drawing Leo's eyes to her feminine form.

"No, no, it's..." Leo struggled to find the right words, his voice filled with awe. "It's... breathtaking. You look stunning."

A soft smile graced Allissa's lips as she spun back to face him, a hint of uncertainty in her eyes. "Help me with the zipper?" She raised her hair, revealing the unfastened zipper and exposing her smooth bare back.

Leo rose to his feet, his hands trembling slightly. The room continued to move around him, but now with anticipation rather than exhaustion. He crossed the room, electric excitement building with each step. Leo placed one hand on Allissa's shoulder and took the zipper with the other. An electric charge surged through his body as he delicately pulled the zipper upward. His fingers brushed against her skin, warm and soft.

"It looks.... great," he whispered, totally unable to find the right words.

Time stood still as their eyes met, reflected in the mirror. The closeness of their bodies ignited a profound connection, an unspoken understanding of the emotions swirling between them.

"Do you think it'll be alright for the party?" Allissa's voice was barely above a whisper, her eyes searching his for reassurance.

Leo's heart raced, and his pulse quickened. Leo surrendered to the intoxicating energy between them. He leaned in, his lips barely brushing against her ear. "Absolutely. You could wear anything and still be... captivating."

A shiver of anticipation coursed through Leo's body as their hands intertwined, fingers lacing together.

The moment was interrupted by a jarring electronic buzz from the intercom system.

"That thing works?" Allissa quipped, her voice a mixture of frustration and humor. She shook her head and stepped away from Leo.

"Clearly," Leo said, letting his breath go. His hands dropped to his sides. "It's probably a salesperson."

"That would be about right," Allissa said, snagging the intercom from the wall. "They always have the best timing." She lifted the phone to her ear. "Hello?" Allissa listened for a few seconds before returning the handset. "Nope, it's still broken. It sounds like a snowstorm through the speaker."

Leo snorted a laugh, trying to dispel the lingering tension. He chided himself for the stupid noise.

Allissa's gaze met his again, and for a moment, they were both caught in a silent exchange of emotions. The atmosphere was thick with unspoken words.

Leo steeled himself, stepped forward and tucked a loose strand of hair behind Allissa's ear, his fingers grazing her skin. "You know," he began, his voice softer than before, "You really are amazing, I..."

The intercom buzzed again, somehow more insistent this time.

A flush crept into Allissa's cheeks, and she bit her lip, a mixture of surprise and delight in her eyes. "You had better see who that is," Allissa said, finishing Leo's sentence. "It might be important. I'll get changed."

With a resigned smile, Leo padded towards the door. Leo took the stairs slowly, his body feeling heavier than usual. His heart raced, and he couldn't shake the lingering sense of positivity that had crept into his thoughts.

As Leo descended the stairs, he took a deep breath, attempting to steady himself. He ran a hand through his hair. With a final, determined exhale, he reached for the doorknob.

"Are you Leo Keane?"

Leo heard the question before he'd even fully opened the door. He saw the faint outline of a person through the frosted glass but couldn't make out their features.

When he heard his name, Leo paused. His anxiety fluttered. His chest became tighter, and he inhaled a sharp breath.

Leo shut his eyes, inhaled deeply, then coughed. His anxiety subsided with the influx of oxygen. During certain periods of his life, such as after Mya's disappearance, his anxiety made him unable to even leave the house. But during other times, such as the last few months — other than the occasional surge — it seemed to have left him alone.

Allowing his anxiety to settle, Leo opened the door.

"Are you Leo Keane?" the man standing outside repeated his question. Before answering, Leo assessed the visitor. He was a short, mousy-looking man, probably no older than Leo. He wore an oversized sweater, possibly dating back at least twenty years.

"Yes," Leo replied, trying to hide the shakiness from his voice. "Who are…"

"I'm… I'm sorry to accost you like this," the man said meekly. He offered Leo a weak and damp handshake. "I need to speak with you as a matter of urgency. It concerns my brother. He's missing and… I… I…"

The warmth from the shared intimacy with Allissa now totally draining away, Leo showed the man inside and up the stairs.

"I'm… I'm… sorry to, you know, take up your time like this," the visitor said, warming his hands on a mug of black coffee a few minutes later. "I wouldn't if it wasn't urgent. I just…"

"It's alright," Allissa said. "First, you clearly know who we are, but who are you?"

"Ah, yes," the man said, grinning awkwardly, before introducing himself as Charles Rolleston.

"Good to meet you, Charles," Allissa said, taking control of the interview. "Now, tell us what's happened, and we'll see if we can help."

Charles took what they all hoped would be a restorative sip of coffee and grimaced at the heat and bitter taste.

"It's my brother Minty." The words came out like a torrent. "He lives in Berlin. He's a fashion designer and has a little shop there. He sells strange clothes to rich people." Charles eyed Leo and Allissa's choice of clothes. "Nothing you or I would wear, I think."

Allissa had pulled on a large hoodie and rolled up the sleeves. Leo glanced at her and suspected that the hoodie might have once — for example, a few minutes ago — belonged to him.

Allissa encouraged Charles with a nod.

"Well, last week, Minty inexplicably disappeared," Charles spoke slowly, worry lacing his voice. "He hasn't returned our calls or messages. I've been in touch with a few of his friends there, but no one has seen him since last Saturday night."

"Could he have gone away for a few days?" Allissa said.

Charles shook his head frantically. "Certainly not. That's not like him at all." Charles dug through his pocket and pulled out a smartphone. "Also, there's this. Minty had a feature on his phone, allowing me and a few other people to track his movements." Charles tapped at the screen several times and placed the phone on the table in front of Leo and Allissa. "This was the last location the phone registered, early in the morning last Sunday. After that it just disappeared."

Leo examined the map and saw a dot showing the phone's location. It was at a train station in central Berlin. The dot was grayed-out, which Leo assumed meant that the phone was now offline.

"How accurate is this supposed to be?" Leo asked, glancing up at their new client.

"I don't know exactly. I'm not an expert, but I think it's good within a few feet," Charles said, turning even paler than before. "I've spoken with the police. They know nothing. Apparently, the security cameras on that platform were down for maintenance. They're looking into it, whatever that means. They say with no sign that Minty's in danger, there isn't much they can do." Charles blinked away the tears that had formed in his lashes.

"Take your time," Allissa said. "There's no rush. We're here to listen."

"I'm worried that... you know... I keep thinking of the

worst possible things. Maybe he fell in front of a train or something." Charles' prominent Adam's apple bobbed in his thin neck. Charles put his cup on the table and dropped his head between his hands. He sucked air between his fingers.

"I'm sorry, I'm sorry," Charles said, regaining control and eyeing Leo and Allissa. "It's just, the location of the phone, and it's so unlike him to do this. He's usually so responsive."

"It's strange, certainly," Leo admitted. "But generally, if something terrible has happened, you would have heard about..."

Allissa gently cleared her throat and threw Leo her trademark *'be quiet and leave this to me'* stare. They both knew that Leo had an ability to say things which sounded insensitive to their clients. Leo shuffled back an inch as though to say *it's all yours.*

"I agree with you," Allissa said softly. "It is a mystery, but I'm sure there's a totally logical explanation. He will be safe and well somewhere nearby."

"That's what the police said, but that's not reassuring. They say they're doing checks, or something. Apparently, they can't escalate it until he's been out of contact for several weeks." Charles sobbed for a few seconds. "We don't need people to tell us he's probably fine. We need answers."

Leo glanced at Allissa. Allissa's expression told him that this would be a great time to remain quiet.

"I don't believe... I can't believe..." Charles took a moment to compose himself, finally looking up at the pair. "Please... can you help?"

5
―――

KASPAR KOENIG KNEW that there was nothing like the kiss of a pistol in the night. The cold pressure of the exterminating snout against your forehead. He recognized it instantly, even before opening his eyes.

What joker is this? He thought. Some troublemakers from Marzhan might have spotted the Mercedes and decided to give it a try. *Fair enough.* Kaspar smiled to himself. It was a nice car. Let them try. They wouldn't get far once they realized who he was.

With his eyes closed, Kaspar tuned in to the sounds. How many of these idiots were there? More than one, surely.

Footsteps shuffled and squeaked across the floor by the door. So, there must be two men at least. That was sensible of them. If the interloper was alone, holding the gun to Kaspar's face would be his last act on this earth.

Kaspar heard the fridge click and rumble. His midnight visitors must have left the door through to the kitchen open. The sound of a passing motorbike thudded into the apartment and then faded. The motorbike sounded distant, which meant the apartment door was shut. That was the right thing for them to do; they wouldn't want a show like this to get interrupted before the interval. These idiots had scored ten out of ten so far. That was all except for their choice of target.

Kaspar could tell quite a lot about a man by the way they held a gun. Inexperienced hoodlums jabbed the weapon at their opponents like it was some kind of bayonet, as though the tip itself was going to cause damage. Kaspar knew that wasn't the way to do it. A gun in a play for power was like a delicate spice. It should be used carefully to bring the dish alive. This guy, Kaspar realized, knew that too.

The cold snout was pressed lightly against his head, enough to let him know it was there, but not enough to put pressure on the holder's forearm. The hand was steady and firm, too. That was good, for his opponent at least.

And if Kaspar wasn't mistaken — he concentrated now — the business end of the gun was thicker than usual. That meant the visitor was using a silencer. The Cold War had finished a long time ago. Nowadays, gunshots drew attention.

Kaspar exhaled slowly. They were doing well but had made one fatal error. Their choice of target. The trespasser had clearly not realized who Kaspar was. Or perhaps they were simply foolish — foolish enough to believe that they could steal from one of Olezka Ivankov's men and escape unpunished. Messing with Olezka was suicide.

As the wall fell, Olezka, a minor criminal, took advantage of the German reunification to establish himself. While others were celebrating their newfound unity, Olezka was establishing trade lines with the Russian Bratva, South American Cartels, and organized criminals across Europe.

Now thirty years on, very little criminal activity

happened in Berlin that Olezka didn't know about. And the *Vor v Zakone* — the Kingpin — was ruthless. Anyone who got in his way was found floating in the Spree. Kaspar had dumped more bodies than he could count in that murky water over the last fifteen years.

These little fools could have their fun now, but it wouldn't last long.

Right, Kaspar thought, preparing to open his eyes. *Let's see what these idiots have got to say.*

"After all these years you thought you could rob from me?" came the voice, as though answering his thoughts.

Kaspar's breath caught in his throat, and his eyes shot open. The room was gloomy. Shards of orange light streamed through the blind and cast horizontal bars on the floor. By this light, Kaspar's worst suspicions were confirmed.

"Olezka," Kaspar said, his mouth suddenly dry. "What are you..."

"Shut up," Olezka replied, his voice gravelly. "Get up. We're going for a drive."

"What? I don't understand. Why are you here?" Kaspar rubbed a hand across his face and blinked. He hoped that the gesture would prove that this was all a bad dream. It didn't.

"Why are you not at home?" Olezka barked. "Get up now. I won't tell you again."

Kaspar scowled, and his vision slowly came into focus. That's true he had borrowed this apartment through a contact he didn't think Olezka knew. Once again, the Kingpin's influence was a surprise.

As his eyes focused, Kaspar not only saw Olezka standing by his bedside, but two other men waiting in the doorway. Kaspar recognized the men, a pair of junior jokers called Henrik and Konstantin. They were part of a new generation making their way through the ranks of the organization. These learned to fire a gun in a computer game, and now thought they knew it all. As far as Kaspar was concerned, they were nothing but pond life.

With a wave of his hand, Olezka commanded a man to switch on the lights. Colors danced in front of Kaspar's eyes for a few moments.

With a tiny movement of the gun's barrel, the Kingpin indicated that his patience was running out.

"Okay okay," Kaspar muttered, his hands raised. "I don't know what you want, but you're making a big mistake here."

Olezka said nothing, his expression as hard as stone.

Kaspar shuffled out of the bed and pulled on the clothes that lay strewn across the bedroom floor. Finally, he took his long coat from the back of the chair and was about to slip it on when Konstantin stepped forward. Konstantin tried to take the coat, but Kaspar kept hold. For a few moments, both men pulled at the garment until a growl from Olezka told Kaspar that arguments were futile.

Konstantin took the coat and checked the pockets. Satisfied that it contained no hidden weapons, he dropped the coat and kicked it across the floor to Kaspar.

Stooping to pick up his coat, Kaspar made a silent promise that when the time came, Konstantin would suffer. With a glance back at the room, and a sense of dread building in his stomach, Kaspar stepped towards the door.

Olezka's men led Kaspar down the stairs and out on to the street. Olezka's Rolls Royce sat double parked at the curb. Henrik and Konstantin forcefully pushed Kaspar into the back of the car, and Olezka joined him. The thugs got into the front, Konstantin driving and Henrik riding in the passenger seat. Konstantin started the V8, and they set off.

Kaspar reflected that in the movies, these things always looked dramatic. People were bundled, fighting all the way from one place to the next. Kaspar knew that, in reality, it didn't happen like that. If someone didn't do what you required, a bullet was promptly lodged between their eyes. No arguments.

6

"I know what you're thinking," Allissa said, closing the door behind Charles and crossing to the sofa.

"What?" Leo said, slumped on the sofa, his arms folded.

"You're going to say that Minty not being in touch for a week is not evidence of anything," Allissa said.

Leo exhaled and sat up straight. "It might not be, but there's a possibility," Leo said while flipping through his notes on the coffee table. "Of course, I'd like to believe that Minty is hiding out somewhere, but in our recent experience, it's never that simple."

Allissa shook her head. "It's never that simple. I feel so bad for poor Charles." Allissa glanced at the door as though Charles was still there.

"Me too," Leo said. "Ultimately, we need to decide whether this is a case we can help with. It sounds to me as though the authorities in Berlin have it in their system and in a few weeks will give Charles and his family the full report."

"You know that's rubbish," Allissa said, dropping onto the sofa beside Leo. This type of case is not considered a high priority. It's like this everywhere in the world. Minty went out one evening and hasn't come home yet. The authorities probably think he's having some kind of jolly sleep over with friends. This is torturous for Charles and his family."

"I agree," Leo said. "We don't know what's going on behind the scenes there..."

"Uncovering the truth of what's going on behind the scenes is our expertise," Allissa said, poking at the notes on the coffee table. "That's our job."

"I agree," Leo said, his tone suggesting he didn't agree at all.

Allissa stared at him, her gaze blade sharp.

"Okay, I don't really agree..." Leo backtracked.

"Don't agree at all, more like,"

Listen, I honestly believe this is nothing like someone going missing on the other side of the world. Berlin is what, less than two hours' flight away. Minty is a capable man who knows the city. He's already lived there for several years. I'm not sure that this is the sort of case we should be taking."

Allissa folded her arms, and the pair sat in silence for almost a minute.

"I do, however, think that the location on that phone tracker gives us enough to say that things might not be as simple as Minty taking some time out." Leo said, almost reluctantly.

"Unless something awful happened to him at that train station," Allissa said.

"Agreed, but then the police would know," Leo muttered, the mystery finally piquing his interest.

Allissa shot him an excited glance. "To answer that, we need to get to Berlin as soon as possible."

Leo let out a long, slow breath as the last part of his reluctance ebbed away. "Yes, okay, I agree," he said.

Allissa swung into action, grabbing her laptop, and thumbing the power button. "There's loads to sort out," Allissa said as the laptop loaded. "I'll get straight onto the logistics — transport and accommodation. You get started with some research. We need to know everything we can about Minty. The more we know, the easier it'll be when we get…"

"There's one thing we need to do before all of that," Leo interrupted, climbing to his feet.

"Ahh yes," Allissa pointed at Leo. "We need to agree on a fee and collect the deposit. We can't be working for nothing, as you always remind me," Allissa said, nodding excitedly.

"Yes, but even before that." Leo grabbed his wallet from the table. "I need to fetch milk. If I'm required to think today, proper coffee is a must. Back in two minutes." Leo spun around and padded down the stairs.

As Leo's footsteps faded, Allissa looked up at the empty room. An hour ago, she'd been trying on her dress for a party she now would not attend. Her right hand slid to her left shoulder, remembering how her fingers had intertwined with Leo's.

The embrace had been unexpected, but Allissa had liked it. Watching their reflection in the mirror, Allissa saw Leo move in to kiss her neck. Instinctively, she'd bent her head to let him in. It felt good. She was ready for it. But then the door had buzzed and…

The computer loaded, interrupting Allissa's thoughts. She shook herself into focus, opened the internet browser and typed *Minty Rolleston* into the search bar.

A list of links appeared, including the official website for Minty's store in Berlin. Allissa tapped that one and spent a few minutes looking through the strange, brightly colored clothes he made and sold for eye-watering amounts of money.

Leo returned five minutes later and set about making coffee. Two minutes after that, he strode into the room carrying two steaming mugs.

"Come and have a look at this," Allissa said, turning the laptop to face Leo. "Minty's clothes are really weird, and very expensive."

Leo placed the cups on the table and dropped to the sofa beside Allissa.

"You got a picture of him?" Leo asked.

"I'll find one." Allissa tapped at the keyboard.

A few seconds later, Minty's picture appeared. Minty looked like Leo had expected. His long hair ran across the shoulders of a maroon blazer. A white shirt, open at the neck, revealed a tangle of chains and pendants, and a large, dark beard contrasted super-white teeth.

"This was taken at an awards night in Milan a few weeks ago," Allissa said, reading the description. "Minty posted it on his social media. Could be worth finding out who he went with."

"Yes, good idea. You've made a good start." Leo raised the coffee to his lips.

"His shop is based in the Kreuzberg area of Berlin," Allissa said.

"What people buy this stuff?" Leo said, looking closely at a bright purple shirt. The garment was made from shiny metallic fabric, which looked more like a chocolate wrapper than an item of clothing.

"No idea," Allissa said. "But I think that really would suit you."

"Life has three certainties," Leo said, holding up three

fingers. "Death, taxes, and I'll never wear anything that ridiculous."

Allissa giggled. "When we've found Minty, perhaps he'll give it to you."

"Absolutely not," Leo said. "You'd have to pay me to wear that."

"How about this? If we find Minty within two days, and he gives you the shirt, you wear it?" Allissa quipped.

"You know that won't happen," Leo said. "So sure, If we find him within two days, you're on." Leo held out his hand and Allissa shook it. The now familiar bolt of electricity moved through him at the touch of their skin.

Allissa moved away and tapped the keyboard. The location of Minty's shop appeared on the screen. "We should check the shop out, too. I'm sure no one will be there, but you never know, something might not look right."

"It's not often we get a case this early," Leo said. "Normally, people come to us weeks after the person's gone missing. We've got a great opportunity here."

"For once we might actually solve the case before it turns into a wild goose chase," Allissa said. "You're going to look great in that purple shirt."

"Three certainties in life," Leo repeated.

"If we can move quickly, I think we've got a good chance," Allissa said. "I'll have a look at flights now. We should be able to get there tomorrow morning."

Leo put the cup down and slid out his laptop.

"No wait," Leo said, "you've got Lucy's party tomorrow. You've got the dress and everything."

"I'll cancel it." Allissa looked at Leo. "I'll tell her something came up."

"No, you can't. You won't. You need to go to that party.

We talked about how it was your way back into the family. You need to go."

Allissa glanced from Leo to the computer. On the screen, a list of flights from London to Berlin appeared.

"She won't mind. I'll call now to apologize." Allissa picked up her phone and paced out of the room. "It's important we get on this right now."

Leo scrolled through some of Minty's social media accounts, trying not to listen in to Allissa on the phone in the kitchen.

Allissa hung up and re-entered the room a few minutes later.

"How did she take it?" Leo asked.

"Alright, I think," Allissa said, shrugging. "I don't think she really understands what work is."

Leo barked out a laugh.

"I'm not joking," Allissa said, deadpan. "My brother is the same, too. They both always got what they wanted. Anyway, I've promised to visit them as soon as we're back, so we will both get to Berlin tomorrow morning."

"Ah shame," Leo said. "I was looking forward to going on my own."

Allissa's mouth moved to argue, but no words came out.

"All you ever do is slow me down, anyway," Leo said, an uncontrollable smile breeding across his face.

7

For a few minutes, no one spoke. Kaspar watched the nighttime streets of Berlin pass in a blur beyond the car window.

"What is this about?" Kaspar forced a laugh into his voice. "Is this some kind of joke?" He glanced at Olezka beside him but got nothing more than a silent stare from the unblinking pistol.

Kaspar clenched and opened his hands three times, his eyes locked on the boss. Despite Olezka's age, he was in good shape. His tall body looked as though it was carved in marble straight from the mines of Kolegamarmor. Even with half the miles on the clock, Kaspar doubted he could take the man hand for hand.

"Am I supposed to have done something?" Kaspar said. "I can assure you, whatever it is, I haven't done it."

The Kingpin gazed out the window as the city streamed past. Kaspar got the message loud and clear — it wasn't time to talk yet.

The further they drove, the sparser the buildings became.

"Look at that," Olezka said, pointing through the window. Beyond the road, a row of rundown warehouses stood while the sky began to lighten.

"What, the buildings?"

"No, not the buildings, you idiot, the sky."

Kaspar looked at the reddening sky, announcing the coming dawn.

"Yes sir, it's getting light."

"You know, there was a phrase I once heard," Olezka said as he looked at Kaspar. "Red sky in the morning is a warning. Or something like that." He flicked his free hand.

Kaspar didn't reply.

"It means that we must be careful today because something bad might happen. You know what I mean?"

"Yes, boss," Kaspar replied. A growing wave of nausea surged through him.

The car slowed and turned from the main road. They passed between two monolithic factories, their walls contrasting against the lightening sky, their chimneys smokeless.

The road became unpaved, and the car bounced. With the tires skidding on the gravel, they continued crawling forward.

Turning again, they pulled into a yard, and the car crunched to a stop.

"We're here," Olezka said.

Kaspar peered out at the building. He thought he knew all the locations Olezka used for his operation, but this one was new. That didn't matter with what Kaspar had planned.

Henrik and Konstantin climbed out of the front seats, each gripping a flashlight. Konstantin opened the door, and Henrik shone the blinding beam of his flashlight directly into Kaspar's face. Kaspar squinted and raised a hand to block out the light.

"Take him in and get him ready," Olezka ordered.

Kaspar stood obediently and straightened up. Although Kaspar was three inches shorter than Konstantin, and about thirty pounds lighter, the brute didn't scare him.

Konstantin snarled, stepped forward, and attempted to seize Kaspar's arm. Kaspar was quicker than that. He flicked his hand upwards and slapped Konstantin in the face. Although the slap wasn't hard, it had the desired effect.

Konstantin, now seething with rage, lunged at Kaspar. Making the first amateur mistake in the book, Konstantin let rage overpower thought. He swung a wild haymaker towards Kaspar's stomach. Although the strike clearly had some power behind it, Kaspar saw it coming a million miles away. It was the typical move that a showman like Konstantin would try. Kaspar sidestepped with ease, and drove a hand into Konstantin's wrist, sending his fist into the car door. The thud boomed through the chassis of the Rolls and Konstantin winced, pain clearly jarring his bones.

Kaspar wasn't done yet. Far from it. In a lightning-fast move, he stepped in close and twisted Konstantin's arm behind his back. The larger man groaned and muttered a string of Russian obscenities. Kaspar pulled Konstantin's gun from its holster, threw it to the ground, and kicked it out of reach.

"Pathetic," Kaspar spat, his grip on Konstantin unyielding. He applied enough pressure to keep his opponent subdued but not enough to cause lasting harm.

Konstantin, struggling and infuriated, attempted to retaliate with an elbow jab, but Kaspar expertly deflected the blow. With a calculated maneuver, Kaspar swept

Konstantin's legs out from under him, sending the bigger man crashing to the ground.

Konstantin hit the pavement, the air whooshing out of his lungs. Kaspar stepped forward and pressed a foot against Konstantin's back, securing his control over the situation.

"Submit," Kaspar barked, his voice icy and unwavering.

Konstantin, panting and defeated, had no choice but to relent. The alley fell into a tense silence, broken only by the harsh sounds of labored breathing and the distant hum of the city beyond.

"Very entertaining." Olezka said, pacing around the car, his gun trained on Kaspar's back. "Now stop messing around like children. Let him go." Olezka's voice dripped with menace.

Kaspar stepped back, reluctantly releasing his hold on the other man. For now, with three against one, he had no choice but to comply.

Konstantin struggled to his feet. Clearly his ego was more damaged than his body. He picked up his gun and levelled it at Kaspar, lacing the move with so much bravado the entire process looked ridiculous. Finally, content that he was in control again, Konstantin scowled triumphantly.

Kaspar lurched half an inch forward and Konstantin reflexively backed away.

"What a pussycat," Kaspar snarled. "Touch me again, and I'll snap your hand off."

8

With Konstantin on one side and Henrik on the other, Kaspar was marched towards the entrance of a derelict industrial building. Kaspar glanced up at the edifice as they approached. Most of the windows were boarded over and lichen covered the bricks.

Henrik strode forward and swung open the door, then Konstantin shoved Kaspar inside. Kaspar staggered into the building, followed by his captors. Right now, he had to play along, as any attempt to flee would be met with a lethal barrage of bullets before he could even take ten steps.

The twin beams of Henrick and Konstantin's flashlights whipped from side to side as they walked deeper into the building. The beams passed across bare concrete walls, illuminating dust particles in the air. As one of the flashlight beams swept across the floor, Kaspar saw a rat scurrying for cover, its fleshy tail swishing from side to side.

"Turn right," Henrik barked.

Kaspar obliged, and the men followed. The flashlights swept through a large room which, as far as Kaspar could see, was empty. Bare concrete walls bore the scars of decay and graffiti. Some windows were bricked up, and others had no glass. The bough of a tree extended in through one.

Kaspar heard the faint whine and thud of a generator, and then the room filled with light. Kaspar blinked as his eyes adjusted.

The room was large, with several concrete pillars. It was empty except for a metal chair in the center. Kaspar saw the chair and felt physically sick. He tried to push the feeling away to maintain his confident, nonchalant demeanor.

"Sit down," Konstantin barked from somewhere behind him.

"You really need to learn some manners," Kaspar retorted. "If I spoke like that, my mother would..." Kaspar didn't finish his sentence. The barrel of a gun thwacked against the back of his head. The room shuddered, but Kaspar did everything he could to stay on his feet.

"Look, you idiot, you're done for," Konstantin whispered. "I would put a bullet in you now, but Olezka wants a word. So, do what you're told."

Konstantin jabbed the muzzle of the gun hard into Kaspar's back.

Kaspar gritted his teeth, rage pounding in his chest like a jackhammer.

"Move now," Konstantin said, leaning in close behind Kaspar. Kaspar felt the man's breath on the back of his neck. Whilst disgusting, the sensation was a giveaway that the amateur was too close. Kaspar grinned. That would be Konstantin's final mistake on this planet.

In one slick move, Kaspar swiped his hand behind him, pushing the barrel of the gun to the side. Konstantin squeezed the trigger but was already a moment too late. The gunshot pierced the air, its reverberations pounding against

Kaspar's eardrums. An already fractured window pane disintegrated into a dazzling cascade of glass.

Kaspar pivoted on the ball of his right foot and swung a lethal one-two combo at Konstantin's head and chest. Clearly not expecting the attack, Konstantin lost his balance. His hands swung backward, and he lost his grip on the gun. Kaspar angled another blow at Konstantin's shoulder, and the weapon went flying across the room.

Henrik turned back from powering up the generator to see the two men locked in a conflict. He raised his weapon, trying to draw a bead on Kaspar, but could not get a clean shot.

Regaining his balance, Konstantin retaliated with a powerful right hook. Still one step ahead, Kaspar ducked out of the way easily. Kaspar swung around and delivered a punishing knee strike to Konstantin's abdomen. As Konstantin doubled over in pain, Kaspar sent an uppercut into his jaw.

With Kaspar sensing the victory, he swung a fist towards Konstantin's neck. Once Konstantin was out for the count, Kaspar considered what he would do next.

Konstantin took a step backward, and Kaspar's fist sailed wide. Out of balance, Kaspar was forced to take a step forward and right into the path of Konstantin's attack. The blow landed hard against Kaspar's ribs and made him wince in pain. Konstantin followed it up with another, slamming into Kaspar's face. Blood trickled from his nose.

Kaspar steeled himself and pushed forward to level the odds. He unleashed a devastating uppercut that struck Konstantin square on the jaw. The Russian gangster's eyes rolled back, and his body went limp. Kaspar stepped up to Konstantin, grabbed him around the chest, and held him up like a human shield.

"I'll snap his neck," Kaspar hissed, spittle flying from his mouth.

Clearly seeing the rage in Kaspar's eyes, Henrik's weapon dropped by an inch.

Kaspar took a step towards Konstantin's weapon. He reached out with his leg and dragged the weapon towards him with his toe. When it was right beside him, he snagged it up and raised it towards the other man.

Henrik, who had only looked away for a few seconds, assessed the scene in shock. The situation had escalated out of control, and he was clearly responsible. Although he raised the gun, Kaspar thought he looked reluctant to use it.

"Well?" Kaspar said. "You wake me up and drag me out here. For what?" His eyes narrowed. This was the worst hangover of the week so far.

"Kaspar, what are you going to do?" Olezka's deep burr came from the door. "Shoot him?"

Olezka stepped into the room, his thick-set body and shaven head cast a bold silhouette against the temporary floodlights. Olezka raised his silenced pistol and aimed at the center of Konstantin's chest.

"What exactly would shooting this man achieve?" Olezka said, as though explaining something to a naughty child. "You would still be here. We would still have the conversation we are going to have. Except he would be dead."

Kaspar pulled a deep breath, looking thoughtful. For now, he wanted to appear as though he were going along with everything the King Pin had to say.

"Dedushka Olezka, you understand I can't have idiots like this pushing me around," Kaspar said, trying to sound respectful.

"I see," Olezka said, nodding his head. He took a step forward, his sweat-dappled scalp glimmering.

"I respect you Dedushka Olezka, I'm just not sure…"

Whisper from Olezka's silenced pistol interrupted Kaspar. Olezka's thick hand merely swayed with the recoil. Kaspar shuddered as the bullet passed neatly through Konstantin's chest. Kaspar let the man slide to the floor, exposing his blood-soaked clothes. The bullet had thwacked through Konstantin's body and missed Kaspar by less than an inch.

"Problem solved," Olezka said, shrugging. "We can't have him pushing you around, can we? The guy was too angry all the time, anyway."

Olezka made a micro adjustment to the angle of the pistol, now aiming it directly between Kaspar's eyes. Olezka's face contorted into a grin. Without even being asked, Kaspar lowered Konstantin's gun to the floor.

"That's good," Olezka said. "We're just going to have a conversation. Is that okay with you?"

Kaspar nodded.

"Henrik, tie his hands," Olezka said. "We can't have any more accidents. Oh, and take Konstantin outside. We'll dump him in the Spree tonight."

9

Watching Berlin slide beneath the belly of the Boeing, Leo thought about the flight he'd taken into Kathmandu. He remembered looking out at the sprawling concrete chaos of the mountain city, and the overwhelming feeling of walking out amongst the noise, the dust, and the oppressive heat.

Berlin looked different; organized and sedate. There were vast open spaces of green, wide boulevards and lazily snaking rivers. It was a city devoid of tall buildings that sprawled into the hazy horizon.

Not only was this city vastly different from Kathmandu, but Leo felt different, too. Back then, he had no idea how to find someone in the real world. But he'd done it, and, he supposed slightly pretentiously, he'd found a stronger version of himself along the way.

The previous night had been a late one. Leo and Allissa had worked long into the night, booking transport, accommodation and reading all the information they could find about Minty and his fashion business. Charles had sent them notes on the correspondence they had with the police, and details about Minty's life in Berlin. With the help of an online translator, Leo and Allissa read the documents. As far as the police were concerned, Minty's disappearance was neither suspicious nor unusual.

As the plane banked to land, Leo glimpsed Allissa beside him. He thought regretfully about the family party Allissa was missing to be here with him. She'd spent two years without her family, and this was her opportunity to reconnect with them. Leo hoped they would get to reschedule soon. Working with families who were missing one of their members reminded them frequently how important family was.

"This way, I think," Leo said, guiding them through the airport half an hour later. They strode toward the train station. It was good to arrive somewhere without the exhaustion of a long and arduous journey.

"Do you know where you're going?" Allissa said, hurrying after Leo.

"I looked it up last night, and I think I remember." Leo bought train tickets from the machine and led the way to the platform.

Ten minutes later, Leo and Allissa sat on the train, rumbling toward the city center. Leo gazed out of the window as they passed the flat industrial landscape of Berlin's outskirts.

Nearing the city, the landscape became more densely packed with modern buildings in glass and chrome, fighting for attention next to Soviet-era monoliths and ornate nineteenth-century domes.

"Let's get off here," Allissa said as they approached Warschauer Street station.

"Our hotel is the next one," Leo said, checking the map on his phone.

"I know, but this is where Minty's phone was last seen. We're passing, so let's check it out."

Leo conceded to Allissa's idea. It would be good to get started straight away. The train came to a hissing halt, and the pair emerged onto the platform. They ducked away from the crowd, surging their way towards the stairs and watched the train rumble away.

"It's unlikely we'll find anything here," Leo said, trudging across the platform after Allissa. "Minty could have passed through here on his way up to the street."

"Agreed," Allissa said. "But his phone stopped working here. That's a reason to check it out if nothing else."

Leo nodded and then did a three-sixty of the station. The place did not differ from the countless other stations Leo had visited in all corners of the world. Several platforms served a multitude of lines, stairs led up to the main concourse and out to the street level. A low bubbling sensation of disquietude rose in Leo's stomach. There was something about this place that didn't seem to fit.

"What are we looking for in particular?" Leo said, glancing around the station.

"I don't know," Allissa said. "Something... that makes us think things aren't fitting together like they should be."

Leo dug out his phone and zoomed in on the location last broadcast by Minty's phone. "On here it looks as though it's on that side of the station, depending on how accurate these maps are." He pointed across at the furthest platform.

A train, heading in the opposite direction rumbled into the station. Its doors emitted a buzzing sound as they opened, and clusters of passengers moved toward the exit. The murmur of their voices and the patter of their footsteps carried across the tracks.

"That would be a good place to start," Allissa said, heading for the stairs.

They walked down to the farthest platform and Leo's uneasy sensation grew.

"Something here doesn't fit," Leo said, glowering down at the platform as they descended the stairs. "There's nothing special about this station. This place is normal. Too normal." He shrugged.

"What do you mean?" Allissa said.

"Minty loves color, right? You've seen the clothes he designs and the way he dresses."

"But that doesn't mean he wouldn't use a station? Everyone needs to get a train from time to time," Allissa said.

They walked out into the center of the platform and Leo checked the map. They were now a few feet from Minty's last known location.

"Of course, but if we're working on the assumption that Minty wanted us to come here and see this, we have to think about why he chose this place specifically."

The approach of an oncoming train pierced the constant hum of the station. Brakes hissed sharply, announcing the train's gradual reduction in speed. Leo turned towards the noise and watched the train slide right over the location where Minty's phone was last seen. A few passengers headed for the exit.

"What I'm saying," Leo said, raising his voice above the staccato of ascending gears as the train accelerated again. "I don't think Minty is leading us here purposefully."

Allissa crossed to the edge of the platform and looked down at the tracks. "It was an accident. Something happened here that..." Allissa's voice dried up in her throat. She stared down at something on the tracks.

"What is it?" Leo said, pacing alongside her.

"Maybe the thing we're looking for," Allissa said, her gaze still locked. Leo followed Allissa's gaze and gasped. On the oil-saturated gravel, its screen cracked and dulled, lay a phone.

10

An hour later, Kaspar sat slumped in the chair with his hands tied behind his back. Olezka and Henrik had left, dragging Konstantin's body with them. Kaspar figured they would roll the corpse in plastic and stash it in the back of the car for disposal later.

Kaspar turned his head from side to side, both assessing the room for the thousandth time, and trying to stop his arms from losing feeling all together. With the floodlights dazzling him, Kaspar couldn't see much of the room. The exhaust fumes from the generator laced the air.

It was typical of Olezka to leave his prisoners in discomfort for some time before speaking with them. This was his way of softening them up, so that when he was ready, the prisoner would confess their crimes without wasting his time.

A few minutes later, although with no way to tell the time, Kaspar wasn't sure exactly how many, he heard the heavy thud of footsteps reverberating down the passageway. Kaspar tilted his head forward and squinted against the blazing lights.

Olezka and Henrik stepped into the room. Olezka removed his weapon and strode towards Kaspar. With Kaspar tied to the chair, the weapon only served as a simple reminder about who was in charge here.

"You know this place used to be a bakery," Olezka said, turning and gazing at each of the walls in exaggerated amazement.

Kaspar yawned dramatically. Olezka loved to go off on tangents when his audience was literally captive.

"Yes, during the Second World War, it was used as a bakery. They used to bake forty thousand loaves a day," Olezka said. "It was all manned by people from the concentration camps. Forced labor."

Kaspar stayed silent, trying to work out how long it had been since this all started.

"A fantastic feat of organization, wouldn't you say? Forty thousand loaves a day."

"Yes, boss," Kaspar said, dryly. "But you didn't bring me here to talk about bread."

Olezka spun around to face Kaspar. A strange smile flashed across his face.

"That is something I've always respected about you." Olezka pointed to Konstantin's blood stain, which had soaked into the floor. "You're not like some of these thugs. You think first and fight later."

"Thank you," Kaspar said, trying to sit up straight. "But I don't think you brought me here to compliment me, either."

"That is also true." Olezka looked hard at Kaspar for what felt like a long time. Dull morning light from one of the cracked windows patterned across his face.

Kaspar watched the other man closely and wondered if the Kingpin had finally lost the plot. Olezka had been running the large and dangerous organization for over thirty years. Maybe the pressure had finally got to him. It was bound to happen at some point.

Olezka snapped into motion. His lips twisted together as though he had eaten something vile. "Whose job is it to collect the shipments from the shop in Kreuzberg?" Olezka asked. "One of the most trusted jobs in the entire organization. Whose job is that?"

Kaspar swallowed. The muscles in his shoulders strained.

"That's my job, boss. I have done that for over a year. Every week without fail."

"Yes, you have." Olezka nodded slowly, like a judge delivering a sentence. "But you see, that's the problem. I spoke with our friends in Lima. Last month, they sent twenty-two packages."

Kaspar nodded and licked his crusted lips.

"But you only brought fifteen to me…"

"There must be some…" Kaspar tried to interrupt.

Olezka snapped his fingers to silence Kaspar. Olezka motioned to Henrik, who drew a laptop from a bag, dragged a chair across the room and arranged the laptop a few feet in front of Kaspar.

"On learning of this discrepancy, first I came to see you," Olezka said. "I was sure there was a simple explanation, and I was ready to hear it. But you'll never guess what? You were nowhere to be found. Your apartment was empty, your phone had been disconnected. No one knew where you were."

"I was taking a bit of me time," Kaspar said. "All work and no play, and all that,"

Olezka spat a humorless laugh, before all mirth dropped from his expression. "As I couldn't find you, I went to see our man at the shop. What's his name… er… Monty…"

"Minty, boss," Henrik offered.

"Ha! What a stupid name," Olezka scoffed. "Why do these British people name their children such stupid things? Has he got a brother called Salty?"

"Not sure, maybe Spicy?" Kaspar offered.

"You know, you are funny too!" Olezka pointed the gun at Kaspar. "But we must stay on topic here. I don't have all day. I went to see Minty and found out that he was nowhere to be seen as well. Now things are suspicious, yes?"

"People go on holiday?" Kaspar offered.

Olezka raised an eyebrow. "Henrik, tell me, do I overreact often?"

"No, boss. I'd say you're quite reasonable, most of the time."

"Most of the time!" Olezka roared, spinning around to face his subordinate. "And what do you mean by that?"

"I mean that... urm... I'm," Henrik stuttered.

"Shut up," Olezka barked, turning back to Kaspar. "I learn both people involved with the missing shipments are not there, so I start to worry. Olezka doesn't like to worry, so I go down the club and see if, maybe the shipments have found their way there without me knowing."

Kaspar swallowed, but his throat felt like he'd swallowed a mouthful of sand.

"And what do I find when I get to the club?" Olezka asked.

"Loud music and flashing lights?" Kaspar offered.

"No! Don't speak unless I tell you," Olezka roared, his icy gaze boring into Kaspar. For several seconds, no one spoke.

"Well? Olezka said, finally. "What do I find at the club?"

"You told me not to speak," Kaspar said. "The secret to good leadership is clear communication."

Olezka charged forward, swung the gun, and smashed

the barrel into Kaspar's cheek. The room shook and blood oozed down Kaspar's face.

"In the club, I find YOU and Monty hanging out together," Olezka bellowed, an inch from Kaspar's face.

"It wasn't me," Kaspar said, wishing he could wipe the blood and spittle from his cheeks. "I was at that apartment. I've been there several days, catching up on my favorite programs."

Olezka clicked his fingers and pointed at the laptop. Henrik powered up the computer and loaded a video recording.

"I thought you might say that," Olezka said. "So, I had Henrik go back to the nightclub and get this."

Henrik hit play, and Kaspar watched a recording of himself and Minty leaving the nightclub. Twenty seconds after Minty and Kaspar ran from the frame, Olezka and another man charged in and gave chase.

"I'd read once that everyone has a doppelgänger, but I didn't believe it until now," Kaspar said.

For the briefest of moments, Olezka looked confused, then he turned towards Henrik and pointed at the laptop.

Henrik hit a couple of keys and zoomed in. A frozen image of Kaspar and Minty filled the screen.

"I meet many people in a lot of places," Kaspar said, shrugging. Cold sweat joined the blood running down his face now.

"Don't lie to me!" Olezka roared, a vein pulsing in his forehead. He waved the gun wildly towards the screen. Kaspar was glad that the gun wasn't pointing at him any longer. "You know exactly what you were doing. You and Mounty..."

"It's M.I.N.T.Y, boss," Henrik interrupted, sounding each letter out individually.

"I don't care!" Olezka bellowed. "You and... that man... were meeting to steal from me."

Olezka's booming voice echoed out, and Kaspar drew a deep breath. "Just say for a moment that is me..." He nodded towards the screen.

"It is you. We can all see that it's you!"

"Well, I'm not sure I even know who that other guy is. What's his name again?"

"Minty," Henrik offered.

"Thanks," Kaspar said, nodding at the other man. "Yeah, I don't even know this Minty fellow. Every time I've been to the shop, the place is empty. I assumed that this Minty is off enjoying spending our money."

Olezka's lips twisted together, compressing his mouth into little more than a grim line.

"And you know that I have business to do in the clubs." Kaspar was impressed with how convincing he sounded.

Olezka's gaze traveled from the screen to Kaspar. Once the eyes were locked on him, Kaspar didn't feel so confident.

"That was the last time Minty Rolleston has been seen," Olezka snarled. "After leaving that nightclub, he disappeared. My contact in the Police says that his family has even been in touch."

"He's probably on holiday," Kaspar hissed. "If that even is him to begin with. As I say, I'm really not sure. I wouldn't recognize the guy at all."

"He steals shipments worth millions of euros and then disappears." Olezka's voice was now little more than a distant rumble.

"What a snake," Kaspar muttered. "Untie me now and I'll help you catch him."

Olezka looked hard at Kaspar. For the slightest moment, Kaspar thought the Kingpin had taken the bait.

"Nonsense," Olezka muttered, more to himself than anyone else. "This guy isn't a crook. He hasn't got the contacts. The only people who have contacts to shift that much product are me..." Olezka stepped across to Kaspar and placed the gun barrel against the top of Kaspar's knee. "...and you."

Panic flared up inside Kaspar. He tried to kick out, but Olezka held him in place with ease. Kaspar glanced down at his leg, his eyes wide with panic.

"I'll ask you again," Olezka murmured. Kaspar felt the other man's breath on his cheek. "Is there something you want to tell me?"

Olezka pushed the gun harder into Kaspar's knee.

"No... I..." Kaspar stuttered a reply.

"Before you answer, consider this carefully," Olezka said, as though explaining something to a child. "If I fire this gun, the bullet will pass behind your kneecap and shred every part of your lower leg. You know this, as it's a threat you have used, and a punishment you have carried out on many occasions."

Kaspar tried to speak, but all that passed his lips was a whimper. Olezka was right. Kaspar knew exactly how painful a bullet to that part of the leg would be. Or rather, he knew how people had reacted after he had shot them in that part of the leg. Kaspar pictured those men now, flopping around like a fish out of water as the white-hot pain consumed their bodies.

"It's incredibly painful, too. Or so I've heard," Olezka continued.

Kaspar gritted his teeth and clamped his eyes shut. He expected his mind to fill with pain. He tensed all the muscles in his body, waiting for the agony which he had inflicted on others in the past, to engulf him.

"I... I..." Kaspar stuttered, his eyes looking wildly around the room. "I took all the packages that were there. I wouldn't steal. Never."

"You are a liar," Olezka said, his voice now a menacing hiss. Then, before Kaspar could say another word, a gunshot boomed through the room.

11

For a few seconds no one spoke. Leo used his phone to check that the locations matched.

"It's certainly in the right place," Leo said, looking down at the device.

Allissa swung off her bag and stepped towards the platform edge.

A bolt of fear shot through Leo's body. He reached out and grabbed Allissa on the arm. "What are you doing?" he hissed through gritted teeth. "You can't go down there, are you mad?" He cast suspicious glances all around. An express train roared by on a nearby platform, as if to emphasize his point.

"I'm going to get the phone, of course." Allissa swung around to face Leo and shrugged his hand away. "This is a lead. It's highly likely, that is Minty's phone. It might give us a clue about where he is now." Allissa's expression was as calm as if the danger of walking on the rails was completely alien to her.

"I understand that," Leo said. "But you can't just start walking around on the tracks. What if an express train comes through or something? That would be that." Leo made a chopping sound with his hands. "Didn't you ever get shown those safety videos at school?"

Allissa tilted her head back and laughed. "You're such a goody two shoes." She reached out and touched Leo on the cheek. "I bet you did everything you were told when you were at school. Did you ever even have a detention?"

The reddening of Leo's cheeks totally undermined the important point he was trying to make. "Maybe... well, no, but that's not the point. Rules like that are there for a reason... to stop you from getting killed."

"I'm going to jump down there and grab that phone. It's five feet away. I'll be back in seconds. You make it sound like I'm going to have a nap whilst I'm down there."

"But we don't even *know* that is Minty's. That phone could be anyone's." Panic laced Leo's voice.

Allissa placed her hands on her hips and stared hard at Leo. "At the very least, it's a coincidence that there's a phone on the tracks at Minty's last known location. We don't accept coincidences. Isn't that something you like to say?"

"Don't use my proverbs against me," Leo muttered, folding his arms. While he hated to accept it, Allissa had a point. "We could find someone, you know, a member of train staff or something. They would go down there and get it for—"

"And wait for hours while they mess around filling a load of forms in." Allissa pointed up at the screen, which showed the arrivals on that platform. "There's not another train for two minutes. I'll be down there and back in less than thirty seconds. Stop wasting time."

Leo looked down at the device again, his feeling of unease growing further. Allissa was right. Locating the phone was a lead, and that was something they couldn't ignore.

"In fact, if you hadn't drawn me into the long conversation about the potential dangers, we'd already have the phone by now."

Leo narrowed his eyes, knowing exactly the point Allissa was making. The feeling Leo had tamed as he entered the station grew. Something here wasn't right.

On the arrivals board, the timer passed the two-minute point.

He huffed out a breath. "Fine, okay. Go quickly." Leo swallowed hard, stuffed his phone deep in his pocket and stepped beside Allissa at the platform's edge.

Leo looked right and left. No trains were approaching, and the platform was empty. To the left, a red signal shone from thirty feet away. A clock suspended from the ceiling counted away the seconds.

"If a train comes, then you..."

"Then I'll lie down and wait for it to pass straight over me," Allissa said, finishing Leo's sentence.

Leo's chest tightened as anxiety tried to take hold. He rubbed a hand across his face and examined the track beyond the station. He couldn't see anything moving down there, at least yet.

Allissa dropped into a crouch and jumped down onto the tracks. Gravel crunched beneath her trainers as she landed two feet from the phone.

Leo's gaze panned frantically from the empty tracks to Allissa, who took a languorous step towards the device. Allissa bent down and picked up the phone. She briefly rotated the device in her hands.

"Don't wait down there!" Leo said, the sweat of tension tickling the back of his neck. "Get back up here."

"Yes, dad," Allissa whispered, the urgency in her voice belied by her calm exterior. She retreated toward the platform. She placed one hand on the edge of the platform and passed the phone up to Leo.

Leo took hold of the grimy device, which was so slippery from the tracks that it nearly slipped out of his hand. Leo tucked it away into his pocket, the greasy residue staining his fingers.

A haunting crescendo of grinding metal rose from the train beyond the station. The sound that clawed Leo's composure into shreds. He spun around, his heart slamming against his ribs, and saw exactly what he feared most — a train tearing towards the station. The train barreled on, now just thirty feet from the station, its headlight burning like an eagle's eye fixed on its prey.

"The train's early!" Leo bellowed, the panic in his voice slicing through all other sounds. "Allissa, get up here now!"

Allissa planted her hands against the platform, the concrete trembling with the vibrations of the oncoming train. A gust of wind streamed into the station, heralding the train's arrival, and filling the station with the smell of hot metal. The deafening screech of wheels against rails filled her ears.

"Move! Now!" Leo shouted, lunging forward. His hands on Allissa's arms with an iron grip.

Allissa tried to pull herself up, but one of her feet wouldn't move. She glanced down to see her sneaker stuck beneath the rail. Suddenly, she paled. She tried to pull her sneaker out, but it wouldn't budge.

"I can't move," Allissa said, panic lacing her voice. She pulled again, trying with every fiber of her being to remove her foot from the vice like grip. It was trapped, wedged immovably between the rail and a misshapen tie.

The merciless vibrations from the onrushing train sent tremors up her leg, a morbid reminder of the impending danger.

Leo's eyes darted from Allissa's terror-stricken face to her ensnared foot. Without a second thought, he jumped down onto the rails, landing with a jolt beside her.

The train's horn tore through the station now, a monstrous two-tone blare. Leo crouched down beside Allissa and saw the source of her entrapment — a twisted piece of metal had stuck into the base of her sneaker like a bear trap.

"Allissa, push down on my shoulders!" Leo yelled over the din. Crouching there, he could feel the train's vibrations working their way up through his knees and into his hips and spine.

The train's horn howled again, more urgently this time. Brakes screeched.

Totally focused on the matter at hand, Leo didn't dare look up at the incoming wall of steel.

Allissa placed her hands on Leo's shoulders and wiggled her foot. Leo pushed his fingers beneath the ensnared sneaker and found the spike. He pushed against the metal and wiggled Allissa's sneaker at the same time. With a grunt of exertion, he heaved, muscles burning with the strain. The metal groaned, a reluctant adversary in this battle of wills.

For a terrifying moment, nothing happened. Then, with a screech of protest, the metal yielded, and Allissa's foot slipped free.

Both glanced up at the train, now nearly upon them.

Leo shoved Allissa toward the platform with all his might. "Climb!" he shouted, his voice drowned beneath in the roar.

Allissa scrambled up, hoisted herself on to the platform

and rolled to safety. Leo stood and, in one swift movement, leaped on to the platform. Leo rolled over, his chest heaving, Allissa's relieved face coming into focus as she crawled to him.

With a screech of brakes and a howl of electric motors, the train thundered into the platform.

Allissa yanked Leo to his feet, their chests heaving, and their eyes wild. Without a word, they turned, and sprinted towards the exit.

12

The shot made the bare concrete walls reverberate. Kaspar's ears whined in protest. He clamped his jaw shut, desperate not to cry in pain. The boom of the shot faded. Kaspar held his breath until the air turned sour in his lungs. Then, surprisingly, he realized that no pain engulfed his brain. He opened his eyes one at a time and glanced down at his leg. He was still in one piece, with no bullet hole.

Kaspar looked up and gazed across the room. Henrik stood with his gun pointed at Olezka, wisps of smoke curling from the barrel.

"I'm sorry, boss. I can't let you do that," Henrik said, his voice a whisper.

"You," Olezka hissed. With respect to the old man, he swiftly grasped the situation. "You two idiots are working together."

"It's time for a change around here," Henrik said, pointing at Kaspar. "Kaspar is that change."

Olezka grumbled something inaudible and reacted at a speed that caught both younger men by surprise. In one slick move, Olezka stepped backward, spun around, and fired several shots in Henrik's general direction.

Henrik saw the old man turning and reacted at the speed of lightning, leaping behind a pillar.

The slugs ricocheted around the room, sending fragments of concrete and dust high into the air, but miraculously hitting none of the occupants. A bullet hit the generator and killed it. The engine coughed, sputtered, fuel glugging out across the floor. With the power cut, the lights died, sending the room into a gloom that looked like the bottom of the seabed. Morning light streaming through the overgrown windows now provided the only illumination.

"Now I see it," Olezka hissed. "It's so obvious to me now. Why didn't I see this before?" He took a step further into the center of the room, his gun pointed squarely at the pillar behind which Henrik was sheltering.

Henrik swung around the pillar and sent a shot in Olezka's direction. Fortunately for Olezka, the younger man wasn't a great shot, and the round went wide. Olezka returned fire. The younger man darted back out of sight.

Kaspar watched the stalemate. Still tied to the chair, he was unable to help.

"I bring you into my organization. I treat you like my own sons. And this is how you repay me," Olezka growled.

Kaspar had to admit, it sounded like the Kingpin was actually upset. A lesser man may have felt pity, but for Kaspar, that was an advantage. Kaspar had learned many years ago that emotional people made rash decisions, and rash decisions rarely ended well.

"You should have retired when you had the chance," Kaspar said, his voice devoid of all sentiment. "If you'd walked away, we would have let you go, but now you're going to have to die."

"Who are you to tell me what's going to happen?" Olezka shouted, his voice booming through the room. "You are nothing. You have nothing."

"I have your missing shipments," Kaspar said, grinning. "And I have your contacts, and soon I will have your entire organization."

Olezka's sentiment boiled over into rage. He swung around and fired two shots in Kaspar's direction.

Fortunately, the chair to which Kaspar was tied was not bolted to the floor. Kaspar kicked down with his legs and heaved his weight to the side. For a moment it looked as though the chair was going to remain upright. Kaspar leaned further, pushing as hard as he could. Kaspar and the chair crashed to the floor, the impact knocking the air from his lungs.

Taking advantage of the distraction, Henrik emerged from behind the pillar and fired three additional shots. The gun howled and projectiles zipped through the air, although still failing to hit anything.

"I'm going to give the lad some shooting lessons," Kaspar muttered under his breath. Although Henrik was loyal to him, the man couldn't shoot a fish in a barrel. Target practice was a priority, starting tomorrow.

Kaspar inhaled to reinstate the air in his lungs. The noxious odor of gasoline filled his nostrils. He glanced across the floor. The puddle of fuel expanded across the floor as it glugged out of the ruined generator.

Kaspar tensed his muscles and tried to shuffle out of the way of the approaching liquid.

"You dare to cross me." Olezka was clearly now so angry that he had completely forgotten Henrik was even in the room. "Now, you will die."

"Hold it right there," Henrik shouted, finally taking a

confident step towards his former leader. "I've got this gun aimed at your back. This time I won't miss." Henrik said.

"I can't guarantee that," Kaspar muttered under his breath. He peered up and saw that Henrik was now ten feet behind Olezka and had a direct line of sight. "Even you should be able to hit that," Kaspar said, again so quietly that no one else could hear. From where Kaspar lay on the floor, both men loomed over him.

Henrik took another two steps forward. For some reason, the younger man was hesitating when it came to finishing the job.

"Shoot him!" Kaspar shouted. "We need him out of the way. There is no way he will go down without a fight."

These young gangsters were too damn merciful, Kaspar thought. In his day you shot first and asked questions later — if there were to be questions at all.

"I will never be out of the way." Olezka's thick lips twisted together in rage. The gun dropped to his side.

"You're a thing of the past, Olezka Ivankov," Henrik said. "It's time for things to change around here... without you."

Olezka shrugged but did not turn and face Henrik. "No way," he barked. "Never."

Henrik took another step forward and raised the gun an inch. He held the gun in both hands and looked down the barrel, focusing on the spot between Olezka's meaty shoulder blades.

"Do it now, quickly!" Kaspar shouted.

"I'm sorry it has to end this way," Henrik said, clearly warming to his theme.

"Shoot him!" Kaspar screamed again, shaking with frustration. "Less of this talking. This isn't Goodfellas. Do it!"

"You will never make the changes we need," Henrik

continued, ignoring Kaspar's pleas. The young man took another step toward his former boss.

Kaspar howled in frustration. The younger man was now drawing too close to Olezka. That could be a mistake, a dreadful mistake.

"You are no longer what this business needs," Henrik continued.

"You think you've got what it takes?" Olezka said, glimpsing the other man over his shoulder. "You think you can do this?" He spat on the floor at his feet. "You two are nothing but rats. I'll show you that."

In one swift motion, Olezka spun around and knocked Henrik's gun to the right. Henrik fired, but the bullet sailed wide. While Henrik was trying to re-aim, Olezka dropped to the floor and rolled to the left. The older man removed a cigarette lighter from his pocket.

Henrik swung the gun around and fired, but Olezka was on the move now. The younger man made the mistake of aiming at where the man was, rather than where he was going to be.

Henrik fired, the slug punched through one of the boarded-up windows, letting a beam of morning light in to the gloom. Henrik spun further to the right, again trying to aim, but Olezka was now several steps ahead.

Olezka struck the lighter, tossed the device over his shoulder in the direction of the puddle of fuel.

Still trussed up on the floor, Kaspar watched the flaming lighter fly. The flame flickered and reduced with the speed of travel but remained ignited. Kaspar swung his feet upward, trying to kick the lighter in the opposite direction. The lighter sailed a few inches above his boot and then, as though it were destined to do so, landed in the fuel.

With a deafening boom that shook the room, the gasoline erupted into a voracious blaze. Flames leaped and danced, licking the air. The fire surged with life, growing larger and wilder with each passing second.

With an incredible effort, Kaspar shuffled himself a few more inches away from the flames. The heat seared his skin and hair as the inferno's fury mirrored Olezka's.

Two of the remaining windows buckled and burst, the shattering sound piercing the roar. Shards of glass scattered like glittering rain. Oxygen rushed in, acting like a shot of adrenaline to the fire's heart.

With a herculean effort, Kaspar wedged an elbow beneath him and used it to leverage himself over and away from the inferno.

With the flames attracting everyone's attention, Olezka spun around and charged for a window. He reached the pane in three steps and barreled headlong through the glass. The window smashed into fragments, and Olezka disappeared.

"Get me out of here now," Kaspar shouted, struggling against the restraints.

The fire churned through the room, charring the walls and ceiling.

Cursing, Henrik dropped the gun and rushed forward. He pulled out a knife and quickly cut the ties that secured Kaspar to the chair. He pulled Kaspar to his feet, and the men ran from the room. As they reached the hallway, a booming wall of flame pounded out behind them.

Kaspar held his breath and ran, his feet slipping over the dusty covered ground. Kaspar muttered to himself. Although Olezka and his organization were on the ropes, the fight was far from over.

13

Half an hour later, Leo unlocked the door to their hotel room and led Allissa inside. The pair had made the taxi journey largely in silence, both wondering what the phone they'd recovered may tell them, and considering how much worse the episode on the track could have been.

"Interesting decoration," Allissa said, pacing into the room and dropping her backpack on one bed. The room was decorated in sixties-style green and yellow wallpaper.

Allissa stepped up to an oversized picture of a middle-aged man hanging on the far wall. "The German Democratic Republic's Minister for Fishing," she said, reading the label beneath the picture. "I'm all for learning about history but having the guy watching us while we sleep is a tad creepy."

"Let's have a look at this phone." Leo dropped his bag, wriggled out of his coat, and drew the recovered phone from his pocket. He perched on the edge of his bed and Allissa shuffled over to sit beside him.

"Turn it on. Let's see if it was worth all that danger." Allissa grabbed at the phone impatiently.

Leo moved the phone out of Allissa's reach and depressed the power button. The screen remained lifeless.

"It's not working," Leo grumbled. "Flat battery, or maybe..."

"Colliding with a train has done it in. Those things are big and move quick. Let me try that." Allissa lunged forward again and successfully grabbed the phone.

"Let's not joke about collisions with trains," Leo said, deadpan.

Allissa thumbed all the buttons and combinations of the buttons, but still nothing happened. She turned the phone around in her hands and examined the screen, which was a spider's web of cracks.

"This person looks after their phone like you look after yours," Leo joked, pointing at Allissa's device on the table, which always had some kind of clumsiness-based issue.

"Hilarious, Mr. Careful." Allissa forced the phone back into Leo's hands. "It might be out of batteries. Let's try to charge it. Tell me you've got the correct cable."

Leo looked at the port on the base of the phone and rummaged through his bag for a charging cable. "It's the same as mine, I think." Leo assembled the charger with the European adapter and plugged the phone in.

Allissa shuffled close beside him, and the pair watched the screen in silence.

"Nothing's happening," Allissa said, after only ten seconds had passed. "Let me." Allissa reached over and wiggled the plug. The pair waited another few seconds, but still nothing happened. Allissa leaned across Leo again, unplugged the adapter and tried fitting it in the plug the opposite way. Allissa eyed the screen intently for another few seconds. When nothing happened, she once again leaned across Leo and wiggled the cables some more.

"Hold on," Leo said, placing a hand on her shoulder. "Let's give it a few minutes without messing around."

With a grumble of frustration, Allissa slumped to the bed. "Maybe it's broken."

"We don't even know that it's Minty's, yet." Leo stared at the phone as though his concentration might have some telekinetic powers. "Woah, hold on," Leo said, sitting bolt upright and pointing at the screen. "Look!"

Something on the screen had changed. Without touching the phone, should it stop working again, Leo leaned forward, squinting. The ghostly image of the charging symbol glowed faintly from beneath the web of cracks. It was as though the light that illuminated the screen had died, but the display was still showing.

Allissa leaned forward, snatched the phone up and looked at it closely. The charging symbol disappeared.

"I don't see anything," Allissa said, replacing the phone on the side table.

"It was there until you started messing with it." Leo went through the process of reassembling the charger assembly. "Don't touch it this time," he instructed when the thing was set up as it had been.

Leo and Allissa stared at the screen for almost a minute. Just as Allissa started to wriggle with frustration, the spectral image of a jagged lightning bolt reappeared.

"There! Look!" Leo pointed at the screen. "Don't touch it for five minutes. Let it get some charge."

As Leo had instructed, the pair held a silent vigil over the phone for almost five minutes.

"Okay, that's enough," Leo said, when they had been waiting in silence for four and a half minutes. As though the phone were some kind of fragile relic, Leo picked it up and held in the power button. The faint charging symbol faded, and, in its place, a ghostly logo of the phone's manufacturer appeared. A few seconds later, the logo disappeared, and a few icons danced in the gloom.

"We're in!" Leo said. Allissa craned her neck and looked over Leo's shoulder. Allissa was so close that Leo could feel her breath on his cheek. He found the sensation of her sitting so close beside him to be distracting, but he also enjoyed it. He urged himself to focus on the task at hand.

Being cautious not to disturb the cable, Leo scrolled through the apps. It was hard to see anything on the screen, but at a particular angle light from the window exposed the faint image.

First, Leo looked at the sent messages. The first message told him exactly what he wanted to know. "This was Minty's phone," Leo said, gravely. Suddenly, the thing seemed to grow heavier in his hand.

Silently, Leo scrolled through the various conversations. Some were about arrangements with friends, and others were about the business. They read all the messages which had been sent and received in the few days before Minty disappeared but saw nothing that suggested he was planning to leave town.

"Try the pictures," Allissa said.

Leo clicked across to the photo gallery. Amid the usual collection of pictures of food, screenshots of so-called funny viral content, and pictures of himself, the gallery was mostly filled with the clothes Minty stocked in his shop. Like the messages, the camera had been used right up to the day of Minty's disappearance but told them nothing.

"Strange," Leo said, lowering the phone to the bed beside them. "It's as if he did drop his phone on the tracks by mistake."

"That's perfectly possible," Allissa said, glancing at her

own beaten-up device. "But that doesn't explain why he didn't go out and buy another…"

"Or just email. This guy runs his business on the internet, he relies on technology every day. I'm sure he has a laptop and probably a tablet, too." Leo straightened up and flexed his shoulders, trying to work out the knot, which felt like it was pulling his shoulder blades together.

"It's weird for sure," Allissa said, lounging back on the bed.

Leo stood up and walked to the window, running the questions through his mind. Their hotel looked out over a small plaza, surrounded by three identical buildings. A few plants struggled out of large pots, and two large bins overflowed.

In one corner, three small children bounced and caught a ball. Leo guessed they were from somewhere in the Middle East. As Leo watched, a woman in a blue hijab appeared at the door of one of the ground floor apartments and waved her flour-covered forearms at the children. The largest child caught the ball, and they ran together, skirting a pile of broken glass and skipping over a rusted bike with one wheel.

Leo smiled. He didn't know the family, but they seemed happy and safe. It was interesting how people came to Berlin for many reasons; some for the fashion, some for the clubs and bars, others for something more fundamental — like safety.

Leo's lips pursed, and his gaze hardened.

"You've figured something out, haven't you?" Allissa said, her chin resting on her chest as she sprawled across the bed.

"Yes, maybe," Leo said, rubbing a hand across his chin.

"Charles told us that the phone was in that location

early in the morning on the day Minty disappeared." Leo turned around to face Allissa.

"Yeah. So, he probably got up early to go wherever he's gone now. The early bird catches the worm and all…"

"Yes, true, or we're looking at it the wrong way around." Leo pointed at Allissa. "Maybe he was coming back from somewhere when he ran into trouble and dropped his phone."

Allissa struggled upright. "That makes sense. His brother said that he'd enjoyed the nightclubs here. There was nowhere quite like them, apparently."

Leo furrowed his brow. "What clubs are there near that station?"

Allissa cracked open her laptop and loaded a map of Berlin. With a few taps, she populated it with the city's nightclubs. There must have been over fifty scattered across central Berlin. "There are loads," Allissa said, dejectedly.

"Focus on those near the station." Leo pulled up a map of the metro system.

"Got it!" Allissa shouted, pointing at the screen. "I know where we need to go now."

14

Olezka stood back and watched as a pair of his men battered in the door to Kaspar's apartment. With a furious look around the hallway, Olezka's rage grew stronger still. There was no way that Kaspar would have been able to afford an apartment in Berlin's Friedrichshain district if it wasn't for Olezka's employment. Olezka had virtually adopted the young German from the streets over twenty years ago. If it hadn't been for Olezka, Kaspar would have nothing.

Olezka's men battered at the door with their shoulders, rattling the light fittings from the walls.

"What's going on here?" Kaspar's neighbor barked, sticking her head out into the corridor. A look from Olezka was all it took to make her disappear back inside and wait for the noise to finish.

Truth be told, Olezka had seen something in Kaspar right from his early days running drugs around the city. Unlike many of the brutes who found themselves in Olezka's employment, Kaspar was intelligent and cunning. He was quick to think and slow to anger, which is what you needed in a trying industry such as this.

Olezka huffed as another crash echoed, the door visibly weakening under the onslaught. Ultimately, Olezka realized, it was Kaspar's intelligence and cunning that had now got him into this mess.

As Olezka watched, the brutish men stepped back from the door and then slammed their bodies against it once again. Olezka silently cursed himself — he should have relied on men like these pair of brutes. Men like these didn't ask questions, they were easy to keep happy, and they did exactly what Olezka told them. For a moment Olezka wondered whether, if he told them to, they would smash open the door using only their faces. Probably, he decided. With a splintering of wood and a screech of the lock and hinges ripping from their mounts, the door swung open.

Unable to stop themselves in time, the men staggered through the door. One gripped hold of the doorjamb and the other collided with the wall inside, sending a gilded framed mirror smashing to the floor.

Raising an eyebrow, Olezka watched the men stagger back to their feet and look around as though trying to work out what had happened. They were great workers; he reminded himself, and men like this would never let him down.

Olezka paced through the door, which now hung at a strange angle on one hinge. Taking a quick look at the mess, he considered moving the door back in position, but concluded it didn't matter. No one would cause them any issues.

"The packages have to be in here somewhere," Olezka said, marching into the hallway. "That villain is running scared. He's on the back foot now and wouldn't have had time to collect, yet. Get searching."

Olezka paced into the apartment's grand living space, his footsteps echoing off the high ceilings and ornate walls. The room, usually bathed in the warm glow of the chandelier, now felt ominously dim. The sheer curtains billowed softly in the breeze from the shattered door.

"You start in the kitchen. You start in the bedroom," Olezka said, turning from one man to the other.

The men nodded and set off in different directions. One of them paused at the wide arch which led through to the kitchen. He spun around as though a thought had occurred to him.

"Urrm, boss, what are we looking for again?"

A shockwave of frustration shuddered its way through Olezka's muscles. "The packages, damn it! Find me the packages that Kaspar has stolen from us. Now!"

Using all his wisdom, the thug didn't ask any follow-up questions, and stalked into the kitchen. A cacophony of smashing plates and banging furniture followed as they both got to work.

Olezka snapped on the light. Glancing up at the chandelier, Olezka levelled a disproportionate amount of anger up at the crystals, which glimmered peacefully above him. It felt to Olezka as though the entire apartment was laughing at him, as it conspired to keep Kaspar's stash concealed.

Olezka crossed towards one couch and flipped it over with a brute force that belied his age. The couch smashed against the wall, sending a framed painting crashing to the highly polished floor. Olezka yanked off the cushions that remained in place and took a knife to the couch's lining. He snaked his hand inside and rummaged around until he was satisfied nothing bigger than loose change could be left in there.

He repeated the process with the other couch and the armchair. Finding nothing, Olezka turned his attention to a grand piano which sat in the corner. Olezka glimpsed his reflection in the piano's polished lid as he approached. Why Kaspar would have a piano in his apartment, Olezka had no idea. He certainly couldn't imagine the man as a whizz behind the keys.

With a grunt, he slid the instrument away from the wall. The legs scraping against the floor sounded like nails on a chalkboard. There was nothing behind the piano. He pushed open the lid and looked inside. Nothing. He upturned the stool, causing a hidden compartment to open. Olezka felt a flurry of excitement as a bunch of sheet-music fluttered to the floor.

Olezka marched back to the center of the room, his heavy boots now crunching over broken glass. Once in the center, he looked around at the destruction. The room was in tatters, and yet Olezka had found nothing. A vein in his neck pulsed in rage.

Olezka went into a full rampage. He tore around the room, smashing tasteful art on the walls, each piece crashing to the ground. The frames splintered, their shards spreading across the floor. He picked up an ornate vase which sat on top of a pedestal and threw it against a wall, but still found nothing.

Enraged, Olezka paced into the bedroom. His man stood amid torn fabrics, smashed glass, and upturned furniture. He'd found nothing, either. Olezka turned back and barged his way into the kitchen. The cupboard doors hung awkwardly from their hinges, their contents spilled out like the innards of a gutted fish. Fine china lay shattered on the floor.

"Found anything?" Olezka said.

His man pulled a series of cookbooks from the shelves.

"Nothing," the man replied.

Olezka grumbled, and his eyebrows shuffled closer together. "There is one more place," he said to himself. "Although to leave the packages there, he would have to either be brilliant, or very idiotic indeed."

15

It was early afternoon by the time Leo and Allissa approached Epitome Nightclub. They strode into a large yard at the front of the building and stopped.

"Are you sure this is it?" Allissa said, peering up at the giant industrial structure which apparently housed the nightclub. Vast rows of shuttered windows covered the front of the building. "This place is enormous. It looks more like a factory than a nightclub."

"It was a power station, apparently," Leo said, fishing out his phone and checking the map. "Yeah, this is the place. It doesn't open until midnight, so we're very early. Apparently, a British DJ duo called the Space Camels are playing tonight."

"Never heard of them," Allissa said, taking a few steps towards the looming structure. "Are they good?"

"Probably." Leo shrugged. "If you like that kind of thing. Maybe we should come back here and see them."

Allissa wandered up to a large graffiti-covered steel door set into the front of the building.

"There might be someone around to set up or something," Allissa said, raising her fist to the door. She thumped hard, but her knuckles barely made a sound against the thick metal.

Leo and Allissa waited for several seconds, but nothing happened. Allissa tried again, but still produced little more than a quiet clunk against the door.

"We should probably come back at opening time," Leo suggested, stepping backward, and scanning the front of the building for security cameras. He saw none.

"What, and wrestle with five-thousand other people to get inside?" Allissa said, pacing across the front of the building. "Let's have a look down here." She pointed down the side of the building.

For a moment, Leo thought of all the trouble they'd run into in their previous cases by exploring unusual places. Noticing his thoughts slipping towards the negative, Leo pushed the doubts away and paced after Allissa. To find out what happened to Minty Rolleston, they needed to get inside this place.

Allissa stepped into a narrow passageway which ran down the side of the building. As with almost everywhere in Berlin, graffiti scarred the walls. Stacks of bottle crates towered against the walls.

Leo glanced at the yard behind them. It felt strange to him that this desolate place became a full-scale party in the evening. He imagined the techno music thudding through the walls as people lined up to enter the building.

A crash of glass bottles reverberated from somewhere down the passageway. Allissa froze and Leo, still focused on his daydream, almost bumped into the back of her.

"What's that?" Allissa whispered, peering into the shadows.

"No idea, but I think it might be our way in," Leo replied.

"Hello, excuse me!" Leo shouted into the gloom. Something moved further down the passageway. "It's times like this that I wish I could speak German," he added.

Leo and Allissa rushed forward and emerged into another small yard set at the side of the building. A pair of double doors were wedged open, and a man rushed into the yard carrying crates of empty bottles.

"Hey, excuse me?" Allissa said, striding towards the man. "Hello!"

The guy turned, and in a moment of imbalance, dropped one of the crates. It crashed to the floor. Bottles skittered and smashed. The guy muttered a series of words, which Leo assumed were German expletives.

"I'm so sorry. I didn't mean to startle you," Allissa said, jogging across and scooping up two of the unbroken bottles.

"What are you doing here?" the man replied, in perfect, although accented, English.

Once again, Leo felt a hint of shame at his own language inabilities.

"We're looking for help with something," Leo said, running across the yard and standing beside Allissa. "We're investigators from England. We're looking for someone who we think was in your club last week."

The man's eyes rolled towards the sky. "We have five-thousand people here, several times a week. You think I will remember this man?"

"You don't have security cameras?" Allissa asked, scooping up two more bottles and slotting them back into the crate.

"You've not been to a nightclub in Berlin before?" The man said, more as a statement than a question.

Leo and Allissa shook their heads.

"No cameras, inside or out. No phones allowed either. It's a different experience here."

Leo felt his hope draining away. "I could show you, or some of your staff, a photo. I know it's a long shot, but anything you can tell us would be helpful."

"I'm sorry." The guy picked up the crates and stacked them on top of the others against the far wall. "I have far too much to do tonight. Three staff are on vacation. I don't have time for this."

He turned and strode back inside, reappearing thirty seconds later with a dustpan and brush. He glanced up at Leo and Allissa as though he'd expected them to have gone away. A flash of frustration crossed his face.

Leo and Allissa snagged up the rest of the unbroken bottles and some of the larger shards of glass. The small act of help seemed to thaw the man's mood just a notch.

"How about we help you," Allissa said. "Our German is non-existent, but we can fetch and carry things."

"All we ask is two minutes with anyone who was here on Saturday," Leo added.

The man straightened up and considered Leo and Allissa through narrowed eyes. "Say, you're not those people that are so desperate to get inside the club that you're trying to trick me?"

"We don't know anything about techno music," Allissa said, almost proudly.

The guy glanced at his watch and nodded. "Alright fine. You can help me re-stock and then I'll help you in any way I can." He extended a hand towards Allissa and then to Leo. "I'm Manuel, by the way."

Manuel spun on his heel and led them through the double doors and into the nightclub. They emerged onto the most impressive dance floor Leo had ever seen. Leo stared up at the speakers which hung from the ceiling and the numerous lights attached to vast gantries spanning the room. Bearing in mind Manuel's comments about phones, he fought against the temptation to snap a picture. That would get them kicked out before they'd gotten anywhere.

"This is room one," Manual said, pointing towards the stage. "This is where the Space Camels will play later." He led them across the room and into a smaller area. "This is the main bar area." Manuel pointed at a stack of crates behind the bar. "I need these empty crates out in the yard, and the new ones brought in from the store."

For nearly two hours, Leo, Allissa, and Manuel shifted the empty bottles out to the yard and then filled up the fridges with fresh ones. It was heavy work and gave Leo a new appreciation of all the cold beers he'd enjoyed in the past.

"Thank you," Manuel said, after they'd finished. The three stood, bedraggled, and sweating, at the bar. Manual snagged three beers from the fridge, snapped them open and passed them around. "I wouldn't have got that done without you. You've done your part of the deal, let me see if I can help you."

Leo dug out his phone and loaded several pictures of Minty. "There are a few pictures there," he said, passing the phone to Manuel.

Leo and Allissa took refreshing swigs of their beers as Manuel looked at the photos. Seeing Minty for the first time, the color visibly drained from Manuel's face. His positive expression of a moment ago melted into a mask of fear. He scrolled to the next picture and became paler still.

Noticing the change, Leo and Allissa glanced at each other.

Manuel flicked to the next picture and nodded slowly, as

though trying to take in terrible news. For almost thirty seconds, no one spoke.

"You recognize him?" Leo asked, finally breaking the silence.

"Come with me," Manuel stepped in close to Leo and Allissa. His voice was now a grave and serious whisper. "We can't talk here."

Manuel turned and paced across the room. He pulled aside a black drape and disappeared into a passage beyond. Leo and Allissa rushed to keep up. Behind the drape, a long narrow passageway ran through the center of the building. About half way down the passage, Manuel stopped, took out a key and opened a door to the left. He disappeared inside, followed quickly by Leo and Allissa.

Manuel hit a switch and an overhead fluorescent tube strobed into life. A desk in the center of the room was strewn with documents, and the walls were covered with posters from previous events.

"Shut the door," Manuel said when they were all inside. "I don't want anyone to walk in on this." Manuel perched on the side of the desk. Leo and Allissa stood against a filing cabinet, both clutching, but not drinking, their beers.

"Last Saturday night, we had an issue here. Two men from a known gang took on two other men. We have an arrangement with the gangs — they do their business here, their men come and go, but they don't cause trouble in the club. That's the deal. Any disagreements must be solved somewhere else."

Manuel fell into silence for a few moments. He looked up at the ceiling as though deciding whether to continue.

"And?" Allissa prompted.

"I shouldn't tell you this, but the man the thugs were after was..." Manuel pointed at the phone in Leo's hand, as though even muttering the words might get him into trouble.

"What happened?" Allissa said, barely above a whisper.

Manuel shrugged. "Honestly, I can't tell you. As I say, I'm sure this stuff happens frequently, but not in here. All I know is that the two gangsters exchanged some blows with two men inside the club, then your man escaped with another guy."

"Do you know who Minty was with?" Leo asked.

Manuel nodded. "I was at the front door when they fled. I remember it well. They pushed their way out of a fire escape, causing a scene. I've seen the other guy around here before, too. He's small and slight, very pale guy, and always wears this long green coat."

"And the men that were chasing them?" Allissa asked.

Manuel placed his hands on the desktop as though steadying himself. "They're bad news. Really bad news."

Leo and Allissa shared another glance, their eyes as wide as coins.

When Manuel spoke, his voice was little more than a hiss. "One of them was a man called Olezka Ivankov. He's infamous." Manuel locked eyes with Allissa. "Listen to me, if Minty is involved with Olezka Ivankov, you need to leave this alone. Do not get involved. Mess with Olezka and you'll be lucky if they ever find your body."

16

"Quickly, get it open," Olezka said as his goons fumbled with the shutter of Minty's shop in Kreuzberg. Olezka stood on the sidewalk, looking at the front of the building. Although Olezka and his organization carried a lot of authority with the police, he didn't want them to get caught breaking into the place out here in the open. It was better that questions weren't asked.

One of Olezka's men removed a prybar from a bag and worked it into the small gap between the shutter and the floor. With the grace of a bull in a china shop, he twisted the lock out of position and the shutter popped loose. The men slid the shutter upward and turned their attention to the door. The men, clearly having learned from their experience at the apartment, worked the end of the prybar between the door and the jamb. They jimmied the thing open in less than a minute.

For a moment, Olezka was impressed. The men marched forward, barging shoulder to shoulder, and blocking the doorway. For a second, they both tried to force their way inside, having not quite worked out what was going on.

Olezka grunted and stepped forward, ready to smash the thug's heads together. Fortunately, they figured it out themselves, turned sideways, and slipped inside.

Olezka groaned, his anger still running high by the disappointment of not finding anything at the apartment. Working on the assumption that Kaspar wouldn't have had the chance to sell the shipments yet, Olezka hoped that by acting quickly they could recoup their losses. Kaspar had been caught in the act and was running without a plan. That meant that if the shipments weren't in Kaspar's apartment, they probably never left the shop to begin with.

Olezka found the light switch and the overhead fluorescent strips flickered to life. The shop was exactly as Olezka had remembered. Clothes in an assortment of mad colors hung from a rail on the right-hand side. On the opposite wall, other garments were folded neatly on display shelves. There were rows of shining jewelry too and a few bottles of beauty products. What need a man had for any stuff like this, Olezka had no idea.

"You know what you're looking for," Olezka said, moving across to a stack of brightly colored shirts. "You in the backroom." He pointed at one man. "You, help me in here."

Both men nodded and set about the assigned tasks. One of them turned to the large table in the center of the room and started rifling through the clothes, the other marched to the door which secured the backroom. He pushed down on the handle and shoved the door. Nothing happened. He tried again but got the same result.

"Boss, the door's locked," the thug said, turning to Olezka.

"Use your special key," Olezka replied.

The thug's face clouded as he thought hard about the instructions. "But boss, I don't have the key."

Olezka placed a hand against his forehead and groaned. He stepped across to the prybar lying on the floor beside the front door.

"Catch this." Olezka threw the prybar at the man, secretly hoping the idiot was too slow to catch it. The thug raised his hand and caught the prybar with surprising speed.

"Got you, boss," the thug said. He turned back to the door and had the thing open in less than thirty seconds.

Olezka turned to the shelves at the side of the shop. He pulled a garment from the top of the pile and held it up. It was a shirt made from some kind of shiny fabric.

"Suits you, boss."

Olezka whirred round to face his subordinate but saw nothing in the man's expression that indicated that he wasn't being entirely serious.

"Get on with it," Olezka bellowed. Olezka crossed to the shelves at the side of the shop and started sweeping all the clothes to the floor. Olezka knew there was a methodical skill to searching for things. He also knew that it was a skill he didn't possess, for the same reason he wasn't very good at interrogating. He was too impatient. He asked the questions he wanted the answers to, and if he didn't get them, he caused the person a lot of pain until they told him.

Olezka crouched down and tore through the clothes that were now piles on the floor. He pulled garments end to end, partly because he feared Kaspar might have split the shipments into smaller packages and wedged them between things, and partly because destroying stuff felt good. When the whole pile lay in tatters, with no sign of what he sought, Olezka crossed to the clothes rail. He wrenched several silk blouses and tailored suits from their hangers, tore them apart, and tossed them on the floor like worthless rags.

Satisfied that those clothes held nothing they shouldn't, Olezka stormed over to the shelves displaying an array of designer shoes and handbags. With a swipe of his arm, they crashed to the floor. He kicked through the pile, his heavy boots crushing delicate craftsmanship without a second thought.

The jewelry stand was next, its delicate necklaces and bracelets sparkling. Olezka smashed the glass with a swift, brutal punch, shards flying like diamonds in a brief, glittering shower. He sifted through the wreckage with ruthless efficiency, gold and silver chains slipping through his fingers.

Olezka straightened up and looked around the small room. They had emptied every box, pulled open and tipped out every drawer. Still, there was no sign of the packages. Olezka sneered. He didn't like people getting the better of him, especially people who should have been loyal.

Olezka paced into the shop's small back room. His associate had already made a good job of the destruction in here. Files of paperwork had been upturned, a whole shelving unit lay on its side, and an expensive-looking music system had been smashed to bits.

"Anything," Olezka barked at the man, who was pulling papers out of the filing cabinet and throwing them up into the air.

"No, boss, nothing," the man grunted in reply.

Olezka kicked a basket of cotton across the floor, several of the balls unfurled, adding to the chaos. He stomped further into the back room, checking beneath and behind things. He flipped the desk in the center of the room, sending a sewing machine crashing to the floor. Eventually

Olezka had to admit that it didn't look like the packages were in here, either.

"What's that?" Olezka said, pointing to a door at the back of the room.

"Not sure," his thug said, shrugging.

"And you didn't think to look?" Olezka paced up to the man, his fists balled and ready. "I told you to search the back room."

"That's not the back room, that's the..." The man's voice was cut short as Olezka slapped him around the head with an open palm.

His rage abating just an ounce, Olezka paced across the room to check out what was behind the door. He grabbed the handle and tore the door open to reveal the shop's small washroom. Olezka huffed out a frustrated breath and stepped into the tiny space.

Although the room was no bigger than a phone box, Olezka set about examining it closely. There was a grubby toilet with an old-fashioned cistern mounted on the wall above it. Olezka stepped on to the toilet and slipped the lid from the cistern. He pulled the chain, and the water drained. Then he looked carefully inside the cistern. Nothing.

Olezka paced back out into the shop. He eyed one man and then the next. "I want twenty-four our surveillance on this place." The men groaned. "If we don't find these packages, I'm holding you both responsible."

17

Leo let the door bang closed behind him and followed Allissa into the bar. It was the first place they'd come across after their chilling conversation with Manuel at the club. Both felt as though they needed somewhere anonymous to talk through what they'd learned and figure out their next move.

Although from the outside the building looked like a run-down townhouse with the render crumbling to expose the bricks beneath and tattered posters flapping fitfully, inside the place was already half full. In fact, the only thing that had hinted at the constant party inside, was the door's small window, which glowed invitingly.

Allissa ordered two beers, and the pair quickly stationed themselves at a table in the back corner. The music and sound of chatting drinkers was comforting. No one nearby would overhear their conversation with this much noise.

Leo slumped into the seat and took a swig of the beer. "I'm just going to say it. I think we need to phone Charles and explain that we can't finish this. I'm totally up for helping people find their relatives, really, I am, but we can't take on the Russian Mafia."

Allissa stayed quiet for almost thirty seconds, sipping at the bottle. "We could do that," she said, finally. "But we've come up against dangerous people in the past and always been…"

"Don't remind me," Leo snapped. "It wasn't even two weeks ago that we had to jump from a building before it exploded."

"I know, I was there too," Allissa retorted.

Leo glanced up at Allissa, his anger immediately dissipating. "I'm sorry, that was harsh. I don't mean to be angry with you. This seems too big for us."

"It's not been a walk in the park, that's for sure," Allissa interjected.

"I know we've taken on dangerous people before, but they weren't gangsters," Leo said, softly now. "All the people we've taken on before have done bad things, but these guys are gangsters. This Olezka character sounds rotten to the core. Being bad is what he does."

Allissa barked out a laugh which turned into a cough as she struggled to swallow her drink.

"What? I'm being serious," Leo said, looking sulkily at the table.

"Sorry, it's not funny, really. It's the way you said that. *Being bad is what he does,*" Allissa mocked Leo's voice. "You sound like you're writing a trailer for a movie."

"That's the problem, though." Leo locked eyes with Allissa, clearly determined not to let the mood lighten. "This isn't the movies. These people are dangerous, and we're not cut out to deal with them." Leo tore part of the label from the bottle and looked down at his hands. "I'd never forgive myself if anything happened to you."

Possessed by some strange force, Leo slid his hand across the table and placed it on top of Allissa's. For a moment Leo thought Allissa was going to move her hand away, but she didn't. The pair sat silent and motionless for almost a minute.

"It's not your job to look after me, you know," Allissa said, finally. "You're not responsible for us. If we get into something dangerous, that's as much on me as it is on you."

"I know that," Leo said, withdrawing his hand and sipping the drink. He looked around the room and noticed a pair of young men drinking a rancid-looking orange shot. Leo's anxiety-filled mood would be the opposite of their experience at the place, where they got drunk and enjoyed good company.

"The question is, how was Minty involved with these badder-than-bad gangsters?" Allissa said.

"Good point. I've never thought about it like that." Leo considered the question for almost half a minute.

"He clearly doesn't have a poor background, he's able to sustain the business," Allissa said. "Why would he have anything to do with people like that?"

"Unless he wasn't able to sustain the business," Leo said, his gaze suddenly hardening.

"What do you mean?"

"We agreed that Minty's clothes looked awful and were really expensive," Leo said.

"Except for that purple shirt you're going to wear when this is all…"

"Let's not even joke about that," Leo said, pointing his finger at Allissa. "I'm stressed enough without thinking about… But what I mean is that I can't see how he can sell that many."

"You're saying the shop is a front? For money laundering or something?"

"It's a possibility," Leo muttered. "Although it could be more than that." He snagged up his phone and did a quick internet search. "Just as I thought, listen to this. The unique selling point of the clothes Minty sells is the fabric they're made from."

"How does that link to the gangsters?"

"It's some kind of recycled cotton and synthetic mix that Minty imports especially from South America. Peru specifically."

Now it was Allissa's turn to sit quietly. After five seconds, her eyes flared as she understood what Leo was talking about. "He's receiving the fabric from Peru. What if there's something else in the package, too." Allissa said, inhaling.

"Drugs, I'd say," Leo said. "Remember Manuel told us that clubs allow Olezka's men to come and go as long as they don't cause trouble, that's their distribution arm."

"And the imports run through Minty's shop as a cover."

Leo and Allissa looked at each other for a long moment.

"I think we've figured out why Minty's disappeared," Allissa said, swallowing the last mouthful of her beer. "It really is amazing how the brain works when powered by this." She held up the bottle and scrutinized the label. "Larger bier hell."

Leo nodded and finished his, too. "As for what's happened to him after that, I think that leaves us with two options. The first one isn't pretty: he's fallen out with Olezka and has been *dealt with*." Leo made quote marks with his fingers for the last two words of the sentence.

"Look at you, already using the gangster vernacular," Allissa jibed.

"Or, he had enough of doing what Olezka wants, and has made himself vanish."

"Let's hope it's that second one. Although, that means he could be anywhere," Allissa said. "I'd say we've got a working theory there. Now we need to work out what to do next. That's a conversation that requires another beer." Without waiting for Leo to reply, Allissa climbed to her feet and strolled across to the bar.

Leo glanced over and watched her in conversation with the server. Although Allissa always seemed to take things like this lightly, worry gnawed away at his stomach like a plague of locusts.

"This place is fascinating," Allissa said, returning to the table with two fresh bottles. "Apparently it used to be a squat, occupied by people with nowhere else to go. Then, over the years, the residents fought off redevelopment and bought it themselves. It's now run by a community of people who work and live here."

"This is a deposit to charity, then?" Leo said, picking up the beer.

"Absolutely, philanthropy tastes good!" Allissa chuckled. "Back to business. What do we know?"

"I think the key to this lies in Minty's shop. That place is the reason Minty is involved with Olezka."

"That's where we need to go now," Allissa said, checking the time on her phone.

Leo nodded. "I think, we should have gone there first." Leo cleared his throat. "Okay, how about this as a compromise..." He looked hard at Allissa as though about to say something he might regret.

Allissa's smile melted, and one of her eyebrows rose in expectation.

Leo took a fortifying sip of the beer. "We will check out

the shop and see where that leads us." Leo prodded the table with a finger. "But we agree on this right now, any sign of Russian Mafia bad guys and we're out of here. We go straight home, with no discussion."

Watching Allissa grin reduced Leo's troubles almost instantly. "Agreed," she said, lifting her bottle. "Any sign of people *who being bad is what they do*, and we will be on the next plane back to London," Allissa said, once again mimicking Leo's voice annoyingly well.

Leo held up his beer, and the pair clinked bottles. He forced himself to smile, although a sickening feeling smoldered in his gut.

18

Leo punched the location of Minty's shop in a taxi app and booked the car. They swallowed the last of their beers, placed the empty bottles on the bar, and strode out into the evening.

"It's not far away," Leo said, standing on the curb. He glanced around and noticed that the building the bar occupied was set around a small park. The other properties around the park gleamed with fresh paint, while the bar looked more like a throwback to pre-unification days. As the door swung closed, the noise of drunk chatter sunk to a murmur. The party was only getting started in this small, clandestine part of Berlin.

"We should come back here when this is all over," Allissa said, glancing at Leo. "We could check out that nightclub for real. It looks like a cool place."

Leo thought about the loud music and hordes of dancers and felt a strange welling of excitement. "You know what? That doesn't sound like a bad idea. I think we're overdue a trip, just for fun."

"Now that's something we can both agree on." Allissa

playfully leant against Leo, sending that now familiar warm feeling spiraling through him. "Actually, though, murdering gangsters aside, we've done well today. We've traced Minty's last few hours, recovered his phone, and have a theory about what's all behind this. Do you think you could have done that on your own?"

"Absolutely, that and more," Leo retorted. "If you weren't here, Minty and I would be enjoying a beer and talking it all through. In fact, we would go to that club tonight to celebrate!"

"Absolutely no way," Allissa said, swinging a playful punch at Leo's shoulder. Leo saw it coming and darted out of the way just in time.

The taxi pulled up, and the pair climbed in the back. From the taxi, Leo and Allissa watched buildings of various designs stream past. Imperial townhouses of white and red jostled for space next to concrete apartment blocks. Creepers climbed the walls and flags hung from windows and balconies.

"Here will be fine," Leo said, ten minutes later as they pulled into the street which housed Minty's shop. They scrambled out of the car and waited for the taxi to pull away before starting down the road. Five-story townhouses lined both sides of the road here. The rumble of the city was quieter too, and listening carefully, Leo heard birds chirping from a nearby park. As though on cue, a pair of blackbirds fluttered past and perched on a windowsill.

Leo dug out his phone and checked the directions. "About one-hundred feet, on the left-hand side," he said.

Leo couldn't help but notice that boutique shops filled the ground floor of almost every building, selling a wide range of items, including clothes, art, and jewelry. Leo wondered whether having a premise in Berlin's Kreuzberg district was a statement of authenticity for creators here, besides a place to trade.

"Let's hope this helps us out," Allissa said, falling into step beside Leo.

"Don't be too hopeful, everything looks closed," Leo glanced through the window of a closed shop as they passed. A dimly lit window display featured rows upon rows of jewelry.

"It's only early evening," Allissa said, glancing at the sky, which was straining from mauve and into purple.

"This probably isn't the time that the fashionistas of Berlin like to open their businesses," Leo said, slightly scornfully.

"They're probably all getting ready to go to the club."

"What a life," Leo muttered. "We're looking for number eighty-seven."

The pair walked in silence for a minute, both counting the numbers.

"Wait a minute, there!" Allissa shouted, pointing down the road.

Leo froze beside her and squinted.

"Five down on the left," Allissa explained. "But something's not right. The shop's open."

The pair hurried the final fifty feet; the shop becoming clearer with every step they took. Unlike most of the others stores, the shutter was rolled up, but the window was dark.

"Wait a second," Leo hissed, grabbing Allissa by the shoulder as they neared. "Olezka or his men might be inside."

They paused and peered through the gloomy windows. No one moved inside.

"We've got to see," Allissa said, breaking away from Leo's grasp. "If anyone is there, we'll pretend to be customers."

Allissa stepped up to the door and tried the handle. The handle clicked as the lock disengaged.

"It's open!" Allissa whispered.

She pushed, and the door swung open, hinges screeching. A bell mounted to the door jangled, the noise sounding strangely eerie as it echoed through the shop.

Allissa turned and locked eyes with Leo. Both knew what the other was thinking. Just days ago, they had walked into an empty restaurant in Hong Kong and almost lost their lives. This, now, was feeling eerily familiar.

"It's not the same as Hong Kong," Allissa reassured. She turned and stepped inside the shop. Then her voice, laced with something akin to fear, reverberated out into the street. "Leo, get in here now."

Leo burst through the boutique's door with urgency, his heart leaping into double time. Allissa stood in the center of the small space, looking from side to side as though she couldn't comprehend what she saw. The once-elegant, high-end boutique had been transformed into a nightmarish scene of total chaos. In the cramped space, designer clothes lay strewn across the floor. Shelves that had once proudly displayed exquisite garments were stripped bare, their contents carelessly thrown about. In the middle of the room, a table that once displayed Minty's creations was now overturned, beside a stack of shimmering clothes.

Allissa took a few steps forward, trying not to tread on any of the clothes. Leo followed, scanning the scene. He glimpsed themselves in a shattered mirror, which cast a fractured image of the surrounding havoc. Leo stepped across to a pile of clothes and picked a garment from the top. It was one of the exorbitantly priced shirts they'd seen on the website, except this one was torn right through the center, as though someone had gone at it in a rage.

A sofa lay on its side at the back of the shop, its plush cushions brutally cut into shreds and, with their filling spewing out.

Allissa paced toward a doorway at the back of the shop. As Allissa approached the doorway, she saw the door lying smashed to one side. The lock had been hacked away from the wood with a hammer or prybar.

Leo dropped the garment back on the pile and joined Allissa. Together, both worrying that they would find something gruesome inside, the pair squinted through the door. With no windows here, the room was completely dark. Leo strained, trying to make out any shapes within the room. Nausea rising in his stomach, the iron fist of anxiety clutching at his chest, Leo searched the wall for a switch. He found one and clicked it on. An overhead fluorescent bulb strobed to life.

In the flickering light, Leo saw that the destruction continued in here. The boutique's backroom, which Leo imagined was typically something of a sanctuary for Minty to create his garments and run his business, lay in a state of disarray which probably exceeded that in the front. A sewing machine lay on its side on the floor, with various parts hanging loose. Rolls of exquisite fabrics, torn and crumpled, streamed from one side of the room to the other.

Amid the wreckage, a battered filing cabinet lay on its side, its drawers wrenched open. Papers and documents had been thrown in all directions. In the corner, a top of the range computer system looked as though it had been thrown against the wall, its screen shattered and stand bent.

"This doesn't look good," Allissa said, throwing Leo an anxious glance.

"I told you these guys were bad," Leo said. He tried to

swallow, but it felt like a golf ball had become stuck in his throat.

"Badder than bad," Allissa added. She slipped out her phone and took a few pictures of the destruction. "You never know. We might need these later."

∽

"Boss, boss, wake up boss!" Volkov shouted, tapping Olezka frantically on the arm. Olezka sat in the passenger seat of their stolen Volkswagen Passat, snoring loudly. Olezka had arranged for himself and Volkov to do the first shift watching the shop and had promptly fallen asleep. To avoid detection outside the shop, they'd stolen a Volkswagen, which was a common sight on the streets of Berlin. What the Volkswagen had in subtlety, it lacked in almost every other area, including comfort.

"Leave me alone. I don't want to!" Olezka grumbled, his lips moving as though chewing something.

"You need to wake up, boss. Someone's gone into the shop." Volkov tapped urgently against the steering wheel. The radio played softly in the background.

"How long have we been here?" Olezka groaned, his voice rough like gravel.

Volkov glanced at his watch. "Four hours and forty-three minutes, but boss, that's not important now. You need to see this."

The inside of the Passat was cluttered with empty coffee cups and crumpled fast-food wrappers.

Olezka opened one eye, followed by the other. He glanced from side to side, looking as though he didn't really understand where they were or why they might be there.

"The shop!" Volkov hissed, pointing at the shop, which was about fifty feet away on the other side of the road.

"What about it?" Olezka grumbled. He shuffled around in the uncomfortable chair and the suspension of the old car groaned.

"Someone has just gone inside."

Now Olezka was awake enough to understand. He shot fully upright, his eyes suddenly alert. "Why didn't you tell me, you idiot?" Olezka slapped Volkov on the arm. He swung open the door, letting some much-needed fresh air inside. "Grab your gun. Let's get in there and finish this."

"No, wait." Volkov said. "It wasn't Kaspar, it was two other people. I've never seen them before." Volkov pressed a few buttons on the long lens camera in his lap and showed the picture to Olezka.

Olezka leaned in and studied the photograph. The picture showed a youngish man with scruffy hair and a mixed-race woman walk into the shop. "I've never seen these people either."

Could they be working with Kaspar, you think?" Volkov asked.

Olezka frowned, still staring at the photograph. "Maybe, although they don't look the type. For now, we watch. Let's see if they carry anything out with them."

19

KASPAR SAT SILENTLY in the Mercedes's passenger seat, smoking a cigarette as Henrik drove them to Minty's shop. Henrik knew the way to the shop, so drove quickly, several times mounting the curb or swerving into the opposite lane to pass slow-moving vehicles.

Kaspar finished his cigarette and flicked it out the window. He reached for his bottle of Club Mate stashed in the cup holder. Club Mate, the magical energy drink made from some crazy root, was one of Kaspar's favorite things about Berlin. Despite his frequent travels, he'd yet to see Club Mate anywhere else.

They sped past a bar, the outside tables already all occupied by patrons and covered with a growing stack of empty beer bottles. That was another thing Kaspar enjoyed about Berlin — there was always a party to be had. And parties meant sales for the recreational drugs, which were his bread and butter.

As Henrik swung the Mercedes into a bend, the chunky tires screeching, Kaspar thought about how Olezka pushed his product on addicts who had no way to repay him. Olezka would encourage his men to give people credit and then exploit them when they were in his debt. These people were addicts, they were ill, and would do anything for their next fix. This sort of business made Kaspar sick. He'd seen lives ruined from the overuse of drugs and wanted no part of that.

He would save his product for the weekend party crew. Those people paid immediately and bought because they wanted a good time — not because they needed to feed an addiction.

The Mercedes swerved off the main road and drew into the quieter streets of Kreuzberg. Kaspar glanced up at a church, its blackened steeple contrasting against the sky. Although Kaspar knew selling drugs was illegal, he felt in his gut that he was on the good side of a gray area. Olezka, bent on his own addiction for power and cash, had strayed firmly into the dark side.

"Turn right," Kaspar said, pointing to the opening of a narrow street on the right.

"But the shop is that way." Henrik pointed down the wide, cobbled street.

"I know, I need to be sure no one has followed us." Kaspar's throat felt dry, and he took another swig of the Club Mate.

Henrik slowed the four by four and turned into the narrow street. They rumbled down the cobbles, squeezing past a pair of overflowing dumpsters.

"Stop here," Kaspar said when they were fifty feet into the side street.

Henrik stopped the vehicle, and Kaspar swung around and looked out through the rear window. Several cars drove past, none even slowing to look down the side street. Kaspar waited a full five minutes before telling Henrik to set off again.

Still cautious, Kaspar led them on a circuitous route through the streets of Kreuzberg. Finally, they pulled in to the road on which Minty's shop was located. Kaspar glanced up at the bulky five-story buildings on either side. A passer-by would have no clue, he thought, finally approaching the shop, the sort of stuff that went on behind these respectable looking shutters.

"Slow down," Kaspar said, as they pulled into the road on which Minty's shop was located. "We don't want to attract any unnecessary attention."

"In this car, you always attract attention," Henrik replied, a grin flashing across his lips.

"Well, I don't want to attract any unnecessary attention," Kaspar said. He wriggled upright in his seat and tipped the last bit of the Club Mate into his mouth.

"I don't know how you can drink that stuff." Henrik nodded towards the bottle. "Tastes like mud."

"Just shut up, and keep your eyes on the road," Kaspar hissed, a cloud passing across his brow. Although he had total confidence in where they'd hidden the packages, going back to the shop made him uncomfortable. This was exactly the sort of place Olezka would know to look.

Kaspar slid out his gun and checked that the magazine was full.

"Are we expecting trouble?" Henrik said.

"We are ready for trouble," Kaspar said, sliding the gun away again. "But hope it doesn't happen."

Henrik spun the wheel, and the Mercedes mounted the curb right outside the shop.

Kaspar wondered whether it would be better to park further away but decided that a quick getaway was paramount. Images of the abandoned bakery, the metal chair and the pooling blood spooled again through his mind. He glanced at the shop and suddenly jerked upright in his seat. His hand slipped back to cover his weapon.

"What is it, boss? You seen a ghost?" Henrik said, killing the engine.

Kasper pointed wordlessly at the shop's front window. Unlike most of the other shops on the street, the shutter was raised. Through the glass, Kaspar could already see the destruction in the gloom.

Kaspar signaled to Henrik that they should both get out and approach the shop carefully. Kaspar stepped down onto the sidewalk, pulled a backpack from the footwell and slung it across his shoulder. The bag was empty, for now, although Kaspar hoped soon it would be stocked with the packages that would set both him and Minty up for life.

He placed a hand across his weapon and stepped towards the shop. Unless absolutely necessary, Kaspar avoided drawing his weapon in public. He was ready to at a moment's notice, though.

Henrik hustled around the Mercedes and took a position a few feet to Kaspar's side.

Both men leaned forward and peered through the window. With the lights off inside the shop, it was hard to see exactly what state the place was in, but things didn't look normal.

Kasper held up a hand, indicating that they should stay motionless. The pair stood for almost a minute, looking for any movement inside. Satisfied they'd seen nothing, Kaspar paced towards the front door. Kasper took the lead and pushed open the door as gently as he could.

A bell attached to the door frame, jangled. Kasper froze, then realizing the source of the noise, continued to pick his way slowly forward. Kaspar made his way through the clothes, which Minty used to sell for a small fortune. It looked as though someone had been through the shop in a mad rage, and Kaspar knew exactly who it was.

"Olezka," he mouthed silently to Henrik.

~

INSIDE THE SHOP, Leo was getting increasingly uncomfortable. "We need to get out of here now," he said, figuring that it was only a matter of time before someone came to check the place out.

"I'm not sure this has helped us learn anything about Minty," Allissa said. She paced across the room, picked up a pile of papers and leafed through them.

"What are you doing?" Leo hissed. "We need to get out of here now. These guys could come back at any time."

"It's not likely," Allissa said nonchalantly. "I don't think they found what they were looking for, and I don't think it's likely they'll come back to have another go." She continued flicking through the papers.

Allissa stopped talking as the bell on the door jangled once again. The sound reverberated through the shop, sharp as a blade.

Leo and Allissa glanced at each other, their blood running cold. Leo took a silent step further into the back room to make sure he was out of sight from the front door.

Allissa's eyes flared with fear, communicating silently that one of their greatest fears was now coming to pass.

Heavy footsteps thumped into the room. A voice followed. Although Leo and Allissa couldn't understand German, they heard a male voice ask a question and another answer.

Leo's heart pounded like a jackhammer, his pulse throbbing in his temples. He took small, shallow breaths, worried that even the sound of his exhaling might betray their presence. Allissa stood frozen, her fingers gripping a sheaf of papers, her face drained of color.

The voices drew nearer as the conversation escalated in tone.

Leo mouthed the word "hide," and pointed at a massive shelving unit which had been pulled away from the wall and split in half. Two large pieces of fabric covered most of the space behind the broken shelves.

Leo tiptoed across the room and slipped, as carefully and silently as he could, behind the shelves. Allissa followed him into the cramped space. Once they were in position, Leo rearranged the fabric to obscure them from the intruders whilst allowing them both to peer out.

They crouched in the confined space, their breaths shallow and rapid, hearts still pounding. Allissa pressed her lips together, her eyes wide with fear. Allissa shuffled in right beside Leo, their bodies tense like coiled springs. The shelving unit's thick wooden frame offered some cover, but it was far from foolproof.

The door to the shop slammed shut, and the intruders paced further inside.

20

In the center of the room, Kaspar stopped and listened. Henrik stood a few feet behind him. Other than the distant noise of traffic, the shop was silent.

Kasper relaxed slightly and let his hand drop from his weapon. Although Olezka had been here, clearly looking for the packages, he wasn't here any longer. Kasper just hoped that their hiding place had been up to the challenge.

"They've done a thorough job," Henrik said, speaking German. "What makes you think they wouldn't have found the packages?"

Kaspar nodded, scowling. He took two steps further forward and did a three sixty. Destruction covered every wall and surface.

"Why did you leave the packages here?" Henrik said, anger seeping into his voice. "I trusted you with my life. Now Olezka will have them, and we are ruined. It's all been for nothing."

Kaspar turned around and grinned at the other man.

"This is not funny," Henrik snapped. "I risked my life standing up to Olezka for you." His fists clenched into balls.

"We needed to sell that to fund the next shipment. Without that, we have nothing."

"You know, my whole life, people have underestimated me." Kaspar pointed a finger at his chest. "I have had to prove myself every day. I have everything planned. Do not worry."

"How can I not worry? Look at this place," Henrik said, his arms stretched wide.

"We have a hiding place that is so good, Olezka will never have found it." Kaspar paced towards the back room. In awkward silence, the pair padded into the small office and workshop space at the back of the shop.

Stepping through the door, Kaspar wasn't surprised to see that the destruction continued in here. The carcass of Minty's sewing machine lay twisted and smashed on the floor and a filing cabinet had been emptied of its contents. For a moment, Kaspar felt nostalgic about the place. He and Minty had spent several nights in here planning their next move or listening to the latest techno tracks on Minty's expensive sound system. Kaspar looked for the sound system and saw it smashed to bits in a heap of wires and circuit boards on the floor.

Kaspar shook himself back into focus and crossed towards the shop's tiny washroom. Kaspar opened the door and yanked the frayed string which operated the light. The bulb strobed a few times before lighting up.

"Where are the packages, then?" Henrik said, his hands on his hips. He peered beyond Kaspar and into the washroom, which was no bigger than a cupboard. The place contained only a toilet and sink. "Olezka has found them, I'm certain of it," Henrik said.

"No way," Kaspar said, turning and locking eyes with the

other man. "The only way Olezka will have found them, is if he knows to push the sink."

"Push the sink?" Henrik said, not at all understanding what the other man said.

Kaspar beckoned Henrik forward and stepped into the tiny washroom. He turned towards the basin, which was mounted on the wall. The thing looked as though it could do with a clean with rust stains blooming across the enamel.

"When Minty and I first discussed this, we considered various places to hide the packages," Kaspar explained. "Many of them were problematic because the packages had to be removed from the shop. We were afraid Olezka might have someone spying on us and catch us taking the packages. Then, Minty told me about this. All you must do, is push the sink."

Kaspar leaned forward and shoved the wash basin. At first nothing happened, then a click echoed through the entire side wall. Kaspar curved his back against the wall and shoved with all his might. A groan of movement rumbled softly. Then, the whole side of the washroom swung inwards.

At first, the gap was an inch, but with some more brute force, Kaspar extended it to six inches and then a foot. He stopped pushing, his face now flushed with exertion, and removed a flashlight from one of the many pockets of his long, green coat. Kaspar clicked the light on and shone it inside the gap. There was a small space behind the wall, big enough to hide a few boxes or even a person in a really cramped condition. Half a dozen brick-sized packages sat inside the hidden space.

"And there is our future," Kaspar said, picking up one of the packages. "Sell these and we are sorted."

"That's incredible," Henrik said, sounding genuinely impressed. "How did Minty know about this?"

"No idea." Kaspar shrugged. He slipped the bag from his shoulders and placed the bricks inside. "Berlin has a history of secrets. Places like this are all part of that." He glanced at Henrik. "Start the car. We can have no more delays."

Henrik obeyed immediately, pacing back through the back room, and hurrying toward the door.

Kaspar took his time loading the final few bricks into the bag. With a value of around one million euros, this haul was certain to set them up nicely once Olezka was out of the picture. Of course, he had hoped that the Kingpin would already be dead and gone, but delays were inevitable.

Kaspar zipped up the bag and swung it onto his shoulder. By the end of the evening, he would have this traded into cash, have Minty paid off, and all things going well, have Olezka out of the scene for good. Kaspar stood, and with one last look around the shop, headed for the exit.

21

Leo and Allissa watched, neither daring to speak, as two men entered the shop. The smaller of the two men led the way into the back room, clearly knowing where he was going. Leo and Allissa watched in astonishment as he opened the door to the washroom and then opened the secret compartment.

Although Leo and Allissa couldn't understand what the intruders were talking about, both heard Minty's name mentioned two or three times during the conversation.

Two minutes later, having removed several packages from the secret compartment, both men stood and left the shop. The man with the green coat snapped the light off as he left, throwing the room into complete darkness.

Leo and Allissa remained still as his footsteps thumped away. The door jangled open and closed again. The noise of an engine rose from out on the street.

Leo was the first to move, heaving the heavy shelving unit from on top of them.

"We need to move, fast!" Leo said, charging across the room. "Do you know who that was?"

"No, but he knew Minty and knew about that secret compartment," Allissa replied, pacing after Leo, and almost losing her footing on a pile of clothes in the middle of the floor.

Leo heard Allissa stumble and spun around to catch her. He clamped one hand on her hip and the other on her shoulder. "When you've quite finished fooling about," he whispered playfully. "That was the man who left the club with Minty. Remember, Manuel mentioned the green coat?"

Allissa nodded.

"If there's anyone in Berlin who knows what happened to Minty, or where he is... that's our guy," Leo said, releasing Allissa after a few moments too long.

"Why are we wasting time, then?" Allissa pushed Leo towards the door. "We need to get after him."

Leo and Allissa sprinted out the door, adrenaline surging. They turned to face a sleek, top-of-the-range off-road vehicle as it reached the end of the road. Its high-performance headlights cut through the twilight, and street lights reflected from the polished paintwork. As the vehicle pulled out, and cut aggressively into the traffic, Allissa recognized the logo emblazoned on the vehicle's distinctive grille.

Leo and Allissa stepped into the middle of the road to get a better view.

"That's a Mercedes G Class," Allissa said, squinting towards the vehicle.

"What does that mean?" Leo said.

"That's good news for us, as they're rare. But it can pretty much go anywhere. Let's just hope we don't have to follow them off-road."

A car horn sounded, causing Leo to spin around. A black sedan — a Volkswagen — accelerated up the road towards them. The driver, a large, angry looking man, gestured impatiently.

Leo pulled Allissa across to the sidewalk and the car sped off. "I've no idea why you know this," Leo said, setting off towards the end of the road. "But come on, we haven't got time to hang about."

Leo and Allissa sprinted to the end of the road just in time to see the Mercedes disappear into the traffic.

"We can't catch it on foot. I know that for sure," Allissa said, her muscles already aching. "Don't start." She shot a glance in Leo's direction. "No amount of running practice is going to help me keep up with a V8 engine like that. We need a better idea now, or they're as good as lost."

Leo slid out his phone and tapped at the screen.

"What are you doing now?" Allissa said, whipping around and piercing him with a gaze.

"A quick game of Candy Crush," Leo muttered. "I'm booking us a taxi, of course."

"A taxi won't help!" Allissa shouted. She spun on her heel as the Mercedes sped out of sight. Luckily, the traffic was bad, and the G Class wasn't too far ahead.

Allissa scanned the street, looking for options. Her gaze locked onto a possibility. Without thinking twice, she surged into a sprint. Her boots pounded the pavement, echoing the rapid beat of her heart.

On the other side of the road, a delivery driver pulled his moped to a stop outside a kebab shop. He placed his feet down and was about to kill the engine when Allissa ploughed into him. The pair rolled to the sidewalk, the poor man stunned by the unprovoked attack. The man, blindsided by the sudden onslaught, lay dazed, too stunned to even cry out.

Allissa shot back to her feet. She leaped on to the moped

and threw back the throttle. The engine howled. Allissa kicked the stand away, the metal clanging against the moped's underside, and then set off.

The delivery driver scrambled to his feet, yelling. He made a grab for the moped, but Allissa pulled out of his reach. She sped across the road, weaving in between traffic and screeched to a stop beside Leo.

Watching her go, the delivery driver sprinted across the road.

"What are you doing?" Leo shouted, his mouth gaping in surprise. "You can't go around stealing things!"

The delivery driver charged across the first lane of traffic. Cars honked, braking at the last moment.

"Do you want to find Minty or not?" Allissa bellowed in return. "Get on!"

Leo's gaze swiveled back to the approaching driver. The man bolted across the second lane of traffic, narrowly avoiding a collision with a taxi. The driver stretched out his hands, clearly ready to make a grab for the bike. Through the visor of his helmet, Leo noticed the man's wild gaze.

Allissa revved the engine, drawing Leo's attention back to her. "Get on now, or I'm going without you."

"Fine." Leo ran around the moped and jumped on the seat behind Allissa.

The delivery guy made it across the road and started sprinting down the sidewalk towards them. He was now a few feet away from reclaiming his moped.

"Hold on!" Allissa said.

"What?" Leo replied.

The delivery guy, clearly predicting that his moped was about to slip through his fingers again, leaped manically forward. His hands swung through the air, ready to grab the bike and take down the thieves in the act.

Allissa pulled back on the throttle. The engine whined and the small bike lurched forward, its front tire leaving the asphalt.

Surprised by the movement, and not yet holding on properly, Leo slid backward, almost falling onto the road. At the last moment, he leaned forward and wrapped his arms around Allissa's shoulders. Leo heaved himself forward as Allissa sped up, pulling their bodies close together.

Allissa sped into the traffic and weaved her way around a series of slow-moving cars. Leo glanced back over his shoulder and watched the delivery guy pull off his helmet and slump down to the curb.

"He's going to call the police for sure," Leo said. "This thing might have a tracker or something like that."

"That's good," Allissa said. "I've got the horrible feeling that where we're going, the police might be helpful."

22

ALLISSA WENT full throttle through the traffic. Clinging on as tightly as he could, Leo longed to turn around and get away from all this craziness.

Leo thought of the significant progress they'd already made. They'd tracked Minty's last known movements, worked out why he might have disappeared and were now on the tail of someone who knew the truth. They had made good progress in less than one day.

"There it is, five cars ahead," Allissa said, her voice pulling Leo back to the present.

The heavy traffic now crawled forward at a little over twenty-miles-an-hour. Allissa skillfully maneuvered the moped between two cars, leaving enough space between them and the Mercedes. The street was a blur of shops and cafes flying past.

Leo leaned out and looked at the vehicle. They were close, but Leo figured that if the traffic opened up, the Mercedes was easily powerful enough to speed away from them in moments.

"Do you really think they'll lead us straight to Minty?" Leo said.

"Probably not," Allissa replied, shouting over the noise. "We both know that things aren't that simple. But it'll be another lead for sure."

"Agreed. Let's get a little closer. We need to make sure we can keep them in sight," Leo said.

"You've changed your mind," Allissa said, throwing him a glance. "I thought you wanted to get a taxi."

"Hey, I want it known for the record that this is all your idea. I try to go through my life without stealing…"

Leo's words were interrupted by Allissa flinging back the throttle and powering past the next two cars in one movement. They shuffled back into the traffic to let a bus going in the opposite direction pass, before overtaking the next car in a similarly reckless fashion.

"That's close enough," Leo said.

Allissa swerved in her lane, barely missing a Volkswagen Passat. The driver of the Volkswagen honked angrily.

Leo glanced around the street as they rolled on. Families now dined in brightly lit restaurants, and groups of men sat smoking outside. Smoke curled upwards in thick white clouds.

Up ahead, the Mercedes indicated and turned at a crossroads.

Allissa saw an opening and sped up to follow. This road, like the last, was broad and busy. Lined on the right-hand side with bars and cafes, on the left, it opened onto a gloomy expanse of parkland. The crowd from a bar overflowed onto the sidewalk. A peal of laughter from a group of men startled Leo as he passed.

The Mercedes bumped up the curb and stopped.

"Don't stop here," Leo said, stealing a glance at the vehicle. "Pass them and park down that side street." He pointed to a narrow opening.

Allissa did what Leo asked, swinging the moped into an alleyway between two restaurants. She kicked down the stand and killed the engine. Allissa slipped a few notes from her purse, unlocked the moped's storage compartment, and placed them inside.

"Two hundred euros for ten minutes rental is not bad at all," Allissa said, locking the compartment and concealing the keys under the front mudguard.

Leo led the way down the street. They paused at the corner and peered out on to the main street. The man in the green coat crossed the road and walked into the park, a heavy black bag draped over one shoulder. The Mercedes remained parked at the curb. Leo assumed that the other man who had been in the shop was still inside.

"Follow him," Leo muttered, stepping out from the side street. "But make it look casual."

Allissa slipped her arm through his and the pair crossed the road. The pair paced up to the park entrance. Leo glanced at the sign, *Volkpark Hesenheide.*

"We're just a normal couple out for an evening walk," Leo said, before his voice caught in his throat. "I mean, we're a normal couple of people. Like a pair..." Leo was grateful that the darkness hid his glowing cheeks.

"I get it," Allissa said, mirroring his pace. "If we are going for a romantic walk, though, you need to stop pacing like a running horse."

Leo slowed his pace to a more casual stroll.

"That's better," Allissa said playfully. "Much more romantic."

Leo blushed again. He wondered whether it was possible that Allissa had picked up on his embarrassment and was exploiting it. He brushed off the thought and focused on the park around them. Despite the darkness, the people of Berlin were still out in force. A man ran past them, his breath billowing in the night.

Leo glanced left and right, hoping to see the man in the green coat somewhere nearby. For now, the gloom held its secrets.

After one hundred feet, the park was almost completely dark. Other than the streetlights, which cast the occasional island of light, gloom hung across the rest of the park. Ahead, a cyclist shot through the lighted pools, like a moth in the night.

Leo saw movement on the path ahead and stopped. He looked hard into the place where he'd seen the movement.

"Got something?" Allissa asked.

"I don't think so. A trick of the light or something. I can't see a thing. He could be anywhere."

They started walking again, slowly.

"He can't have gone far," Allissa said. "We saw him come in here two minutes ago."

On either side of them, the park's lawns sprawled out. They took another few steps forward and then both froze. Several voices came from somewhere nearby.

"There," Allissa said, pointing forward. "About twenty feet ahead. There's a group of people."

Leo could make out a group of ghost-like figures. One figure held a lit cigarette, its flame flickering in the air like a firefly. The night hung like a cloak around the figures. Leo heard movement. It was close, but he couldn't see it. He resisted the urge to use the light from his phone, as that would give their location away immediately.

Something moved again, closer this time. Then, a figure

materialized from the gloom. It was a tall, thin man whose eyes glimmered from some distant light. Leo looked the man up and down. It was certainly not the man they had followed.

"Möchtest du etwas?" the man said in a hushed voice.

Somewhere behind the man, Leo sensed more movement.

"I'm... I'm..." Leo stuttered, his voice weak. He breathed deeply. He tried to control the panic which burned his chest and stung his vision. Suddenly, he wanted nothing more than to run away.

Clearly sensing Leo's fear, Allissa tightened her arm around his. "We're looking for someone," she said.

"You want something?" The man spoke again, switching to English. "Hashish? Charlie?"

"No, I..." Leo's thick tongue stumbled over the words. "We're looking for someone," Leo repeated.

Another figure moved, swaying towards them through the trees. Although the figure was just a shape in the gloom, the height and build were right.

"We're looking for a man named Minty Rolleston," Allissa said, her voice loud and clear.

"You want drugs?" the man repeated.

In the gloom behind the man, Leo saw the figure had stopped moving.

"We're looking for a man called Minty Rolleston," Allissa said again. "His parents sent us to find him."

A light appeared, slicing through the night. The beam swung around and then focused on Leo and Allissa. Leo blinked, dazzled by the beam as the holder of the light took a step forward.

"How do you know Minty Rolleston?" came a voice with a thick German accent.

The surrounding shadows made it seem like shapes were melting and forming.

A smaller man materialized from the gloom, a flashlight held high.

"His parents have sent us to look for him," Allissa said.

"His family sent you?" The German's inflexion didn't make it clear whether it was a question or a statement. Leo nodded, still dazed by the bright beam of the torch.

"You come from Brighton?" the speaker asked. Closer now.

Again, Leo nodded.

A bike clattered past them. Although its rider was invisible, the light attached to the bike's handlebars illuminated the man for a moment. Leo got a flash of the green coat, the thin pale face, the closely cropped hair.

"Yes, we come from Brighton," Leo said.

"Minty's parents sent you?" the man asked again. Leo found the man's use of Minty's first name reassuring. The muttered words that followed reassured him further. "He said that they would be worried about him. I can see why…" the man trailed off.

Leo focused on the man.

"Well?" the man said, snapping his focus back onto Leo and shaking the torch. "Minty's parents send you, yes?"

"Yes," Allissa replied.

The man in the green coat thought for a while. "What's the name of his brother?" He said, as though trying to catch them out.

"Charles Rolleston," Leo replied. "He came to see us a few days ago and told us they were worried about Minty. I'm here to find out what happened to him."

"I don't believe you," the man snapped. He pointed the beam of light directly into Leo's eyes. "I think you are working with Olezka. Is a very clever plan. Get an Englishman to pretend to be looking for Minty, get inside and report back. Very clever. But not clever enough."

Allissa glanced anxiously from Leo to the man and back again, thinking about what to do if this turned nasty. Dashing for the cover of the nearby bushes would probably be for the best, although there was no knowing how many people their captor knew nearby.

"Wait," Leo said. "Listen to this." Leo scrolled through his phone and selected the recording he'd made from Charles' answerphone. "This is the message Minty left on Charles' answerphone on the night he was supposed to have died."

Leo pressed play. Minty's voice strained from the phone's small speaker, followed by the voice of their captor. The beam of light held steady. Minty's voice on the recording trailed off and the noise of the rumbling train rose to distortion levels. Everyone exchanged glances, clearly wondering how the situation would end. "We're here for answers," Leo said. "His family is very concerned."

"We get our answer, and we're gone," Allissa added. "Whatever business you've got going on here is not our concern."

The man shot Allissa a glance, as though he'd totally forgotten that she was there.

"You are alone?" He said, finally.

"Yes," Leo said.

In one swift move, the man grabbed Leo's bicep and started pulling him back towards the road.

"What? Wait, where are we going?" Leo yelled.

The German stopped and spun around to eye Leo and Allissa. "We are going to see Minty Rolleston, of course."

23

For Minty, lying low really was frustrating. Where he'd usually be able to go to the shops on a bright afternoon or meet friends for drinks, now he was confined to the house.

It wasn't as bad as actually being dead, he supposed, as it was only for a couple of days. So, it was definitely a lot better than being medically dead. Death being, well, permanent.

The days felt like they dragged on forever. He couldn't go out. Couldn't contact anyone. Couldn't do anything a living person might. But it wasn't for long — that's what Kaspar had promised.

He wasn't even allowed to go online, nor contact his friends and family.

Minty sighed and stared at the woods behind the house. The thick new leaves sparkled in the bright afternoon sun. He couldn't even go for a walk outside. Minty crossed the room and collapsed onto the sofa. *It's the doing nothing,* he thought, drumming an erratic percussive pattern on his knees. He couldn't do *nothing*. He needed to do *something*.

But what?

He glanced around the room and saw the large screen TV and expensive music system. Sure, he could put some music on, or even watch a film, but those things were at best a distraction, or at worst a danger. He was concerned that the music could either mask the sound of the alarm on the front door or draw the neighbors' attention.

It wasn't safety, or boredom, that troubled Minty, though. Sure, being on edge was bad, but it was the thoughts of his family that haunted him the most.

A car engine groaned from the street outside. Minty was suddenly alert. He looked around the room, holding his breath. When the car drove past and its sound faded back into the city, Minty tried to relax once again.

Minty closed his eyes and tried to picture his family — his brother, mum, and dad. His eyes shot open again when he couldn't help but focus on the expressions of worry which were etched into their eyes. He couldn't help but feel raging guilt over the worry they must be feeling. All he wanted to do was make contact and tell them he was alive and well. One call would be enough.

One more frustrating thing was that Minty had been ready to leave Berlin for weeks. The car, which he'd bought using cash from a man in Spandau, was packed and ready. Minty had chosen it especially to get them out of the city unnoticed; a cheap and inconspicuous ten-year-old Volkswagen.

Minty had even planned a series of destinations on an old German road map he'd found on the bookshelf.

The waiting was the hard bit. This wasn't just waiting, though. This waiting for a man with half a million euros.

The burner phone which Kaspar had given Minty vibrated on the coffee table. Minty drew a sharp breath and answered the call. There was only one person it could be. "I have the money," came Kaspar's voice. "You know where to meet me. One hour." The line went dead.

24

THE MAN PULLED Leo back through the park at a speed that belied his size. Allissa rushed alongside, worried that if she lost sight of Leo and the man, she may not find them again.

In less than two minutes, they stepped back out on to the road, Leo and Allissa breathing heavily from the exertion.

"Get in the car." The man in the green coat released Leo's arm and pointed at the Mercedes four-by-four, which was still parked on the opposite side of the road. The man paused for a few seconds, looking one way, and then the other. To Allissa, it appeared as though the man was worried about being followed.

Leo glanced around too, his instincts telling him to run. His eyes sought safe options, from the gloomy park to a nearby crowded restaurant. To Leo, both these places were better than going with this man who he didn't know, or trust, and had been involved in Minty's disappearance. Leo felt Allissa's fingers close around his shoulder. The gentle touch instantly brought a sense of calm. Leo spun around and locked eyes with Allissa. Her gaze told him what he already knew — they needed to go with this man, otherwise they may never know what happened to Minty Rolleston.

With the reassurance that he wasn't facing this alone, the panic thumping in Leo's ears muted. He tuned into the noises of the city once again. Music thudded from the bar across the road and traffic growled down the street. Although the evening was drawing on, Berlin was just getting started.

Clearly satisfied that no one had seen their exit from the park, the man in the green coat stepped out into the traffic. He strode across the road, causing two cars to brake aggressively. One driver protested on the horn, although they quieted down after a stern glance from the man in the green coat.

Watching the man stride across the road, the green coat billowing in his wake, Leo realized that despite not being tall — at least a foot shorter than Leo himself — the man had some kind of aura about him. There was an air of calculation and menace in his movements and behavior.

The man in the green coat reached the Mercedes. He swung open the door, again obscuring a car that was trying to pass, and climbed up into the passenger seat. The man signaled that Leo and Allissa should get in the back.

Allissa led them across the road, waiting for a slightly larger gap in the traffic and swung open the door. The pair slid into the Mercedes' luxurious interior. Leo pulled the door shut and the noise of the city sunk again. The car smelled of tobacco smoke and sweet air freshener. Leo noticed the driver examine him in the rear-view mirror. Leo looked away, breaking the stare.

The man in the green coat muttered a few urgent sounding German words. The driver clicked the Mercedes into gear, swung the wheel, kicked down on the gas, and powered out into traffic. A bus behind them flashed in frustration. The aggressive acceleration forced Leo and Allissa to sink into the soft upholstery. Scrambling back upright and searching for the seatbelt, Leo wondered why these men always seemed to move at such a dangerous and frantic speed.

"What's... where are we going?" Leo asked when they were rumbling forward.

Without replying, the man in the green coat fished a packet of cigarettes from his pocket. He placed a cigarette between his lips and lit up. After he'd taken three long drags and exhaled through the open window, the German finally answered. "We're going to see Minty, as you asked."

"What is this all about?" Allissa asked. "What is Minty involved in?"

The German gazed out at the passing city and remained silent for several seconds. Allissa was about to ask again, when finally, he spoke.

"They used to say that the night was darker in the East, but I'm not sure anymore," speaking softly. The German took another drag on the cigarette, another cloud of smoke drifted out through the window. "I have lived in this city my whole life... I have lived here and worked here. I feel like I have fought my own battles for this city."

They reached a gap in the traffic, and the driver punched the accelerator.

"But it's time for a change around here," the German said, exhaling again. "They say the wall came down when the Soviet Union crumbled all those years ago. But, with people like Olezka still running things, we are still under their control. We must make a change." He paused for a slow and thoughtful drag on his cigarette. "Even beneficial change can be painful. We Berliners know this more than most." He stretched out his arms as though visually indicating how big the deceit was. He suddenly snapped out of the reverie and spun around to face Leo and Allissa in the rear of the SUV. "I'm sorry. How rude of me. I have not even introduced myself. I am Kaspar, and this is Henrik." Kaspar pointed at the driver and then, with the cigarette clamped between his lips, he extended a hand towards Leo. Leo took the hand and introduced himself. Kaspar's grip was firm and dry. Allissa did the same.

Henrik glanced at Leo and Allissa in the rear-view mirror and nodded. Leo found the icy gaze to be more unsettling than comforting.

"Henrik is the best driver in Berlin, that I can guarantee you," Kaspar said, gazing proudly at the other man. "Some people merely drive, but Henrik he is a master of the road." Kaspar took a drag on his cigarette. "Now we are all friends," Kaspar said.

Leo didn't feel so sure. He glanced at Allissa, whose gaze was now as hard as steel.

"You are here to help Minty, so we are on the same team," Kaspar said. "All will soon become clear." Kaspar muttered some words to Henrik, and they both laughed.

"Where are we going?" Leo asked again. Through the window, the buildings of the city had thinned out into suburban sprawl.

Kaspar rubbed his hands together. The cigarette remained clenched between his teeth, ash now sagging from the end. "We go to a place that no one will think to look," Kaspar said. "You will see that Minty is safe and well. Then you can reassure his family that all is good and soon he will be back with them."

"Where is Minty?" Allissa asked.

Kaspar flicked the half-finished cigarette out and raised the window.

"You know the best place to hide a grain of sand?" Kaspar said, grinning. His gaze panned expectantly from Leo to Allissa. Both shook their heads. "On the beach, of course. Minty is in a place that no one will ever find him. They wouldn't even think to look."

Kaspar turned and exchanged some words with Henrik in a language neither Leo nor Allissa spoke. Although Leo had thought that both men were German, it didn't sound as though they were speaking German. Kaspar laughed for a moment, before sinking into silence.

"Why did he need to disappear?" Allissa asked.

"You will see, my friend, you will see. All will be explained. You have nothing to worry about," Kaspar repeated. "Before we get there, I have some work to do. No more questions, please." Kaspar clicked on the reading light above his head, pulled a bag from the footwell and placed it on his lap. "Pass me that bag," he said to Leo, pointing at another bag in the center of the rear seat.

Leo passed the bag forward. From the weight, it felt as though the bag was empty.

Making no attempt to hide what he was doing, Kaspar opened the first bag and removed a giant bundle of Euro notes.

Leo and Allissa eyed each other in surprise. From their position and in the low light of the four by four's interior, it looked as though the bundles were fifty-euro notes, and at least an inch thick. Leo made some quick calculations, and estimated there were at least fifty thousand euros in each bundle.

The German flicked through the first bundle of notes,

checking that everything was as he expected. Satisfied he counted them out at an impossible speed.

Watching the process, Leo could only imagine why someone might carry that much money around.

Kaspar counted out bundles in silence, placing each bundle in the second bag. When he'd counted out the required amount, Kaspar zipped up the original bag and stuffed it beneath the passenger seat. He did up the second bag and placed it on the floor between his feet.

"What's that money for?" Allissa asked, unsure whether the question was pushing their luck.

Kaspar spun around and looked at the pair, a mischievous glimmer in his eye.

"That is for Minty. Enough there for him to start again wherever he wants. A fresh life." Kaspar wiggled his fingers as though he were a magician performing a trick.

Kaspar's gaze drifted to the window behind them. The muscles in his face hardened, and his eyes focused on something through the window. He pointed aggressively at a car behind them. His previous gray pallor became an angry red.

"We are being followed," Kaspar snarled. "I knew they were suspicious. But to follow me?" Kaspar swung around and thew Henrik a glance. "We must lose them. Lose them now!"

25

Minty looked at himself in the mirror and groaned. He used to take so much pride in his appearance — appearance used to be everything — but right now, his reflection was nothing but a disappointment.

Gray and ashen, he looked as though the apprehension of his situation had drained life from him. His eyes, which used to be bright and engaging, were now red and sunken. He rubbed a hand across his face and blinked hard. It would all be over soon. It would have to be.

Even his hair, which used to shine, now hung bleak and lifeless. *Maybe there's some rough justice in this,* Minty thought, turning the woolen hat between his fingers. The thing that he'd always been proud of — the way he looked — was being taken from him.

Minty pulled the hat down over his hair and paced towards the back door. Swinging a black jacket from the back of a chair, Minty promised himself that when this was all over, he'd never lose touch with his family again. He zipped the jacket and stepped back to look at his reflection in the mirror. Gone were the colors he used to love wearing.

Tonight, though, wearing black was essential. Tonight, he needed to move in the shadows.

That won't be for long, though, Minty thought. As soon as this was over, he could once again be the brightest person in the room.

Minty paced through the house and let himself out the back door. He slipped through the garden, keeping to the shadows as much as possible. Reaching the end of the garden, he opened the gate and slipped into the woodland. He glanced back at the house. In an hour, all going well, he would be back here. Then Minty could move on and never come back.

26

HENRIK STAMPED on the gas and the powerful G Class, which had been purring softly up to that point, surged forward like a wild beast unleashed. The sudden acceleration pressed Leo deep into the plush upholstery of the rear seat. He gripped on to the armrest with all his strength, as though he were likely to fall from the vehicle completely should he let go.

Allissa, who had turned around to look through the rear window, was forced across the rear parcel shelf by the acceleration. She reached out and pushed herself away from the rear windshield. She struggled back into her seat and glanced at Leo. The pair locked hands across the rear seat.

In the front seat, Kaspar's face contorted with urgency. He shouted and gesticulated wildly. "We must lose them!" he yelled. "They cannot follow us!"

Leo's eyes darted between Kaspar and Henrik. He cursed himself for getting into the car, and now being thrust into a perilous gangland car chase. Adrenaline coursed through his veins, and the pit of his stomach fell to the floor.

Henrik hit the brakes and threw the wheel to the right.

The Mercedes slewed across the road, tires screaming under the pressure.

The motion forced Leo into the door. Allissa slid across the seat and collided with him. Every muscle in Leo's body tightened, and he fought to catch his breath.

Henrik expertly brought the wheel back and hit the gas. He worked the gear shift like a race car driver.

Allissa scrambled up again and peered through the rear windscreen. A black sedan zoomed around the corner, a hundred feet behind, and sped up like crazy. The pursuing car slipped into the oncoming lane to overtake some slow-moving cars, before darting out of the way of oncoming traffic. Whoever was behind the wheel of the sedan was driving with calculated precision and no regard for anyone else on the road.

"Who is that?" Allissa said, shouting over the howl of the Mercedes' V8 engine.

"There's only one person who that can be," Kaspar said, his finger jabbing towards the blazing headlights which were now gaining on them. "Olezka."

Kaspar leaned forward and pointed towards an intersection a few hundred feet away. "Don't stop," he snarled.

Leo gazed at the intersection which they were barreling towards at incredible speed. A traffic light hung above the road, a green light currently illuminated.

Henrik accelerated hard, his foot pinning the pedal to the floor. The needles on the dash swept upward and into three figures. The engine howled as the revs slid deep into the red.

Leo gripped Allissa's hand again and braced himself. Something bad was about to happen, he could tell.

When they were fifty feet from the intersection, the green light disappeared, replaced by amber. Leo glanced at

Kaspar, whose smirk was now illuminated by the sickening hue.

Time slowed to a crawl as the traffic light transitioned from orange to red. The asphalt, the waiting cars, and even Kaspar's pale face were bathed in the color.

"Don't stop! Don't stop!" Kaspar shouted, pointing aggressively at the intersection.

Leo watched the bright lights of the pursuing sedan strobe through the rear glass. Stopping for the traffic light wasn't a great option, either. Leo saw something that caused dread to sweep through his body.

A truck pulled out into the intersection. The truck moved slowly, accelerating from a standing start and belching clouds of diesel fumes up into the air.

For a moment, Leo thought Henrik might apply the brake. He didn't. Henrik's hands remained locked on the wheel, his gaze focused on their diminishing options.

If anything, Leo realized, they were still speeding up. With twenty feet of road now remaining before the intersection, stopping was no longer an option. Leo sat frozen in the seat, his heart beating with the same ferocity as the four-by-four's pistons. Allissa's grip tightened around his hand.

The truck picked up speed, moving further into the intersection, now almost completely blocking their way.

"Brace yourselves!" Kaspar shouted.

Henrik downshifted through the gears. The engine bellowed at a whole new level of noise.

The Mercedes roared into the intersection, heading straight for a collision with the side of the truck. Leo pictured the resulting mangled mess of the two vehicles. Even though the G Class was a large vehicle, the truck would come off better.

Henrik swung the wheel to the right. Tires howled

again, as though deciding whether to obey. The Mercedes teetered, swinging one way and then the next. Finally, the vehicle obeyed, barreling to the right, its body lifting on to two wheels.

The Mercedes screeched across the road and swerved around the truck with inches to spare. The truck jammed on its brakes, shuddering to a stop in the center of the intersection. Horns blared and lights flashed.

Henrik deftly spun the wheel, winding them on to the open road on the other side of the intersection. And then, as though nothing happened, he hit the gas again.

Allissa and Leo exchanged a look that conveyed more than words ever could.

"Ha! That will show you!" Kaspar turned around and shouted at the rear window. He pumped a fist in the air.

"It's not over," Henrik said, pointing in the mirror.

Leo spun around in his seat and watched the sedan pick its way through the stationary vehicles now blocking the intersection. Once it was clear, the sedan sped up again, already eating up their hard-earned lead.

"I've got an idea," Henrik shouted. "Hold on!"

Leo and Allissa did what they were told, just in time.

Henrik stamped on the brakes, leaving streaks of rubber on the asphalt. The Mercedes swung into a residential street. Large trees lined both sides, blocking out the glow of the occasional street lights. The Mercedes' headlights whipped from side to side as Henrik swung them around cars parked along the narrow road.

Leo watched the narrow street sway from side to side through the windshield and hoped they wouldn't meet anything coming the other way.

Ahead, the road straightened up, allowing Henrik to speed up again.

Leo turned and glimpsed their pursuers. Although they were still giving chase, it looked as though Henrik's plan was working. The sedan was less maneuverable than the Mercedes and had been forced to slow through the suburban chicane. They had finally gained some ground.

Leo turned his attention to the road ahead. They shot past a sign indicating that the street was a dead end. Leo was about to argue, when Henrik hit the brakes and swung the wheel to the right. The Mercedes went into a full sideways skid. Henrik skillfully feathered the brakes, stopping from spinning totally out of control at the last moment. Henrik swung the Mercedes around so that they were facing back in the direction they'd come.

"I don't think this is a good idea," Leo muttered, his eyes pinned on the corner around which their pursuers were about to emerge. "They will be here any—"

27

"Catch them," Olezka bellowed, slamming the dash with a fist. As usual Olezka wasn't driving, but for once he wished he was.

The man in the driving seat, Volkov, was coincidentally the thug who'd got his face smashed in by Minty Rolleston's bottle in the nightclub. Olezka knew Volkov was looking forward to some revenge for the gash that was still yet to heal on his cheek.

Volkov stamped on the gas, sending their five-year-old Volkswagen Passat into a frenzy. Olezka had chosen the Passat — freshly stolen with fake registration plates — because they needed to blend in while observing. Olezka's Rolls Royce would stand out like a beacon on the grimy streets of Kreuzberg.

Although the car served the purpose, Olezka did wish his men hadn't stolen one that smelt so bad. Whatever the legal owners did in the vehicle, it wasn't nice. Right now, though, Olezka had much bigger things to worry about.

"We searched that shop! How is it possible that there

was still something in there?" Olezka moaned for the tenth time since they'd set off.

"I don't know, boss," Volkov muttered. "We should have taken them down before they got to the park."

Olezka scowled. In hindsight his subordinate was right, although Olezka had liked the idea of Kaspar turning the packages into cash ready for his collection. Plus, making a move like that in a busy part of the city always led to problems. The last thing Olezka needed right now was losing his profit in police bribes.

"Shut up and concentrate," Olezka hissed, throwing Volkov an ice-cold glance. "We end this now, and all is good."

The Mercedes G Class swerved into a narrow residential street, revved up, and kicked up dirt on the road.

"Yes, I know that road!" Olezka pointed excitedly at the Mercedes. "That's a dead end. They'll get nowhere down there. They've just sealed their fate."

Volkov mashed the gearbox, and the Passat whined under the strain. Used to school runs and trips to the supermarket, this car clearly wasn't up to the job of a full-scale chase.

"It won't matter. They've got nowhere to go," Olezka hissed.

They reached the turn, and Volkov swung the wheel hard, barreling the Passat into the corner. Volkov suddenly saw their problem and hit the brakes. Ahead, the narrow road had been turned into something of a chicane with cars parked outside the houses on both sides. He eased his foot on to the brake to avoid smashing into either of the cars.

"Don't slow down!" Olezka roared, hammering on the dashboard. "They're getting away!"

Volkov hit the gas, and the Passat squealed off. At a

reasonable speed, he wove them easily through the first set of cars and swung into the turn for the next two. Now, with their speed increasing, the turn was more difficult, causing the Volkswagen to lurch from side to side.

Olezka gripped the handle above the door and swore in his native language.

The next vehicle, a large motorhome, stuck out almost halfway into the road. Volkov eased on the brake to make sure they got around without a collision.

The reduction in speed irked Olezka more. He sent another series of thumps into the dashboard, splitting the plastic in two.

Beyond the motorhome the road was empty, so Volkov confidently stomped down on the pedal. The Passat's engine screamed in protest. Volkov pushed harder, driving the car far beyond its mechanical limits. The vehicle's frame shuddered with the strain. Volkov gripped the wheel tightly, ready to finish this chase once and for all.

Olezka pulled his gun from its holster and gripped it tightly in his gloved hand.

The road ahead widened and curved to the right. Volkov increased their speed even further.

The Passat rounded the corner, and the road ahead opened, revealing something neither man expected. Volkov's grip tightened on the wheel and Olezka shot upright in the passenger seat, his head almost colliding with the ceiling.

The Mercedes G Class sat fifty feet ahead, pointing back in their direction. The four-by-four's headlights blazed like the eyes of a predator fixated on its prey.

Volkov wavered between the gas and the brake, not knowing what to do. Olezka scowled, not offering any advice.

The Mercedes' powerful engine roared to life, and the vehicle charged forward like a bullet from the barrel of a gun. Volkov's gaze flicked to the rearview mirror for a split-second calculation — no escape but forward. The gap closed to a breath's width; time slowed to a crawl.

∼

INSIDE THE MERCEDES, Kaspar silenced Leo's concerns with a flick of the wrist. All eyes remained riveted on the approaching lights, which now danced around the corner. At a speed which bordered on insane for such a narrow road, the Volkswagen shot around the corner. The driver was clearly desperate to regain the progress they'd lost.

Leo saw two large men sat inside the sedan, their furious expressions illuminated in the dashboard's lights. Seeing the Mercedes now stopped in the center of the road, the men's expression morphed from one of frustration to one of anger.

In the momentary distraction, it looked as though the Volkswagen was heading straight for a parked car. The driver reacted, although a moment too late. The sedan jerked into the middle of the road, fishtailing wildly. The sedan lurched to the right and then to the left, screaming and crunching as the tires smashed against the arches. Finally, the driver got the sedan under control, and they crunched to a stop.

"Amateurs," Henrik muttered, clearly enjoying the inferior driver's mistakes.

Henrik hit the gas, and the Mercedes pitched forward. He swung the wheel so that they were heading straight for the Passat and accelerated hard.

Leo watched in the glow of the dazzling headlights as

the two men in the sedan realized what was happening. The driver groped around in panic, obviously undecided whether to hold his ground or get out of the way. Leo remembered noticing a bulky set of bars mounted across the Mercedes' front grill, meaning the four by four would come off far better in a head-to-head collision.

Henrik moved up through the gears. He kept them in a straight line. If the Volkswagen didn't move, they were going to ram it from the road.

Leo grew tense as they neared, now looking down over the smaller car. He gripped on to the seat in front and prepared himself for impact.

For a moment, Leo thought Henrik was going to spin the wheel and get them out of the way, but he didn't. With nerves of steel, the German held the wheel firm as they charged towards the smaller car.

The Volkswagen's driver, looking up at the larger vehicle, which clearly wasn't slowing, suddenly lost his nerve. He threw the Passat into reverse and kicked down on the gas. The Volkswagen howled, its tires slipping across the street. The sedan slid out of the path of the Mercedes with half a second to spare. With a crunch of twisting metal and shattered glass, the Volkswagen smashed into a parked car. The alarm squealed and lights flashed.

Henrik howled in amusement at the other driver's feebleness and adjusted their course. The Mercedes swung to the left, bumped up a curb, and roared down a narrow pedestrian path which Leo hadn't even noticed was there.

28

Olezka swung forward and then backward, his face twisted into a snarl so ugly he didn't really look like a face at all. Shattered glass now filled the back of the car, and the screeching of the car alarm would soon attract the attention they really didn't want.

The Mercedes sailed past the front of the Passat with a few feet to spare. Olezka even saw Kaspar in the passenger seat, flicking him a crude gesture. The Mercedes turned to the right, bounced up a curb and disappeared into a narrow pedestrian path towards the forest.

Olezka tried to speak but was too angry for words. He turned to Volkov and was about to reward the idiot with a bullet to the side of the head, when he saw a man hurry from a nearby house, no doubt drawn by the shrieking alarm. The last thing Olezka needed right now was a dead bystander. Things like that always made the worst sort of headlines.

"Follow them, now!" Olezka pointed his gun toward the fleeing Mercedes, which was now only visible by its lights.

Volkov didn't need to be told twice. He slammed the

Passat into gear and set off, another crunch of metal reverberating through the chassis as they pulled away from the other car.

∼

Bushes and trees whipped the sides of the Mercedes as they shot down the footpath.

Henrik clicked a switch on the dash, and a set of lights attached to the vehicle's roof blazed, lighting up the path fifty feet ahead. They passed between the houses which lined the residential street and emerged into a woodland. The four-by-four's thick tires making good progress on the uneven ground. Henrik didn't even need to slow. Densely packed trees shot past on both sides of the path.

Henrik glanced in the rearview mirror. In the distance, the lights of the Volkswagen gave chase, although they were still some distance behind.

Leo and Allissa gripped the armrests in an attempt to avoid being thrown around inside the vehicle.

The roof mounted lights sliced an arc through the gloomy forest, showing that the path curved sharply up to the right. To the left, the forest ran down a slope, the bottom of which Leo couldn't see.

For a few minutes, the Mercedes climbed up the winding gravel path. Although Henrik slowed their progress to stay on the track, their vehicle, with its off-road tires, was far more appropriate for the track than the following Volkswagen. If the sedan made it up here at all, it would take the driver several long and frustrating minutes.

"Here is perfect," Henrik said, nodding to a clump of bushes at the side of the track.

Kaspar nodded in agreement.

"What are we doing here?" Leo asked, his voice shaking after the hair-raising journey. "They're still after us. Can't we just get out of here?"

"You'll see," Kaspar said, throwing Leo a hard glance, which made it clear than no further questions were required.

Henrik drew to a stop and reversed behind a row of trees. Once in position, he switched off the lights, plunging the vehicle into darkness.

Slowly, Leo's eyes adjusted to the forest. He could make out the dim shapes of the trees and a gentle glow from the sky.

They didn't have to wait long. Two minutes later, lights whipped furiously through the shadows. The beams swung around, casting angular and chaotic shadows.

The sound of the sedan's straining engine rose about the gentle patter of the idling Mercedes.

Kaspar leaned forward and peered hard into the forest. "Wait," he whispered.

The sedan lurched further on, picking its way up the incline. Gravel skittered from the track as the Passat's tires spun, barely keeping a grip on the incline. The brightness of the sedan's lights increased even more as it approached the last turn.

"Quiet," Kaspar whispered, totally unnecessarily, as every person inside the car was focused on their approaching pursuers.

The shadows danced and strobed more wildly now as the sedan neared, lurching from right to left. Leo saw the sedan emerge. He saw the brutes inside, their expressions masks of pure frustration.

The sedan struggled on, sliding from one side to the other, and spraying grit in all directions. After several long seconds, the smaller vehicle pulled directly in front of the concealed Mercedes. For almost two seconds, the sedan continued climbing and nothing happened. Then, Kaspar spoke.

"Now," he whispered.

Henrik hit the gas, and Kaspar clicked on the lights. The four-by-four shot forward, slamming into the side of the sedan.

Leo watched the men inside whip around to face their attacker. Their skin blanched as they realized what was going on. The driver fought with the controls and the passenger tried to swing open the door.

Metal crunched against metal as the Mercedes' bars slammed into the side of the sedan. The door buckled, twisting it closed. The driver struggled, trying to push open the door in vain. Windows shattered.

Henrik pushed the Mercedes harder, each of the chunky wheels digging into the track.

The driver of the sedan revved the engine and tried to pull them away. The tires howled across the track, tearing the gravel away and slicing through into the fresh earth.

Henrik buried the gas pedal again. The engine growled like a caged beast finally unleashed. The sedan slid across the path and teetered on the edge. The hillside rolled away below them for fifty feet, punctuated by trees like a deadly game of pinball.

The sedan's driver tried desperately to break loose. The vehicle heaved and skidded, its wheels spinning desperately, but achieving nothing.

Henrik pushed them forward another two feet. Gravity started doing the work, pulling the sedan down the slope. The sedan slid slowly at first, but soon picked up speed, dragging mud and fallen logs with it like an avalanche. For several seconds the sedan slid unhindered, then a sickening crunch resonated through the wood as the sedan struck a tree. The impact forced the vehicle around, facing back up the slope.

Leo watched the driver, desperately trying to control the car in any way possible. The spinning tires sprayed mud and leaves in all directions but achieved nothing. The sedan slid backward a few feet before smashing into another tree. This impact swung the vehicle hard to the right. The sedan slid down faster and faster until a collision with a fallen tree forced the vehicle into a roll. The sedan spun over twice and disappeared behind a web of bushes with a bone shattering crunch. Smoke rose from the vehicle like a ghostly surrender.

Henrik reversed them onto the track. He applied the brake, and they all peered down at the battered Volkswagen lying on it's roof and partly obscured by the bushes. One of the battered car's headlights remained illuminated, casting strange shadows through the trees.

"Wait for it," Kaspar said, pointing at the stricken vehicle. "I know it's going to happen."

Leo was about to ask what they were waiting for when a bright tongue of flame leaped from the car. The flame danced around the underside of the engine for a few seconds before igniting with a thump. The explosion roared through the forest, sending a fireball skyward, searing through the canopy, and leaving a blackened scar in the serene woodland.

"And that's why you don't mess with us," Kaspar said, pointing animatedly down at the crumpled sedan. "Now, we can meet Minty."

∼

THIRTY SECONDS EARLIER, as the world outside the Passat turned into a blur, Olezka braced himself. His muscles coiled like springs, and his mind kicked into survival mode. He knew they hit several trees on the way down but wasn't sure where or what direction they were pointing. When the car finally came to a stop, Olezka took a moment to work out where they were. The car, he figured, was upside down. He checked himself for injuries and miraculously, found none. His body ached, but that was nothing. He was alive, conscious, and ready for revenge.

Olezka released his seatbelt and crashed down onto the interior of the roof. Shards of glass dug into his hands as he worked himself around and crawled towards what would have been the passenger window. Struggling, he pulled himself out through the gap, his hands throbbing, and finally got to his feet. By the flickering of one of the Passat's lights, Olezka saw his gun lying on the roof below where he had fallen. It was lucky that the thing hadn't been thrown from the car as they'd fallen. Olezka bent down and picked it up.

"Help, Olezka, help me." Olezka heard a weak voice from inside the car.

He peered inside and saw Volkov still hanging upside down, his face a mask of blood. In the gloom, Olezka could hardly see the man, but knew that things didn't look right.

At that moment, a flame flickered from the Passat's engine.

"Get me out of here, please!" Volkov screamed, shaking feebly. "Olezka, you have to help!"

Olezka glanced at the man and considered his options. In one sense, he thought the man was an idiot who could burn in the car for all he cared. In another, he didn't know what the rest of the evening held and could probably do with the backup.

Ultimately, as usual, Olezka's business mind won. He scrambled back inside the car and tried to pull off Volkov's seatbelt. Olezka thumped the button, but nothing happened.

"It's jammed," he muttered, beads of sweat now running down his forehead.

Olezka glanced up at the car's hood. Thick smoke belched out, cloaking the one working headlight. It wouldn't be long until the whole car went up in flames, and when that happened, Olezka didn't want to be anywhere nearby.

Olezka groped around at his hip and found the knife he always carried fastened there. With a couple of quick swipes, he cut through the seatbelt. Volkov thumped down, sprawling across the ceiling.

Olezka grabbed the other man by the collar and dragged him out through the shattered passenger window. Olezka pulled Volkov up to his feet. Fortunately, neither man had broke any bones in the collision. Olezka dragged Volkov away as the ferocity of the flames increased. When the men were about twenty feet away, the flames engulfed the whole car.

Olezka released Volkov, and the men staggered, their joints loosening with the movement, behind a sturdy pine tree. A moment later, the explosion ripped through the forest. Even from twenty feet away, Olezka felt the wall of heat wash over him. He turned back and watched the flames consume the car, licking up into the forest's canopy.

Olezka turned his attention up to the roadway, which curved out of sight fifty feet above. He pointed at the twinkling lights of the Mercedes as it drove away and then turned to Volkov.

"Once again, they underestimate us," Olezka growled, pointing at the Mercedes' taillights. "Wherever they're going, it'll be close. The tire tracks will lead us straight there. All we must do is follow." Olezka spun around and eyed his subordinate. "You better be ready to finish this, otherwise you can go back in the fire,"

"Yes, boss," Volkov said, wiping his face. "I can run."

29

Henrik revved the engine, and the Mercedes continued climbing up the track. After their earlier pursuit, progress now seemed easy.

In the back seat, Leo rolled his shoulders and tilted his head from side to side trying to remove some of the tension. He felt as though the pursuit on the road and their mad dash through the forest had rattled him to the core.

"Who was that?" Allissa asked. "What did they want?"

"That was Olezka." Kaspar casually tugged out another cigarette. "Unfortunately, we could not finish things as quickly as I'd hoped. But that problem has now been solved."

Leo blinked and saw in his mind's eye the inferno consume the Volkswagen once again. Although the men inside were clearly bad guys, that would still be an awful way to go.

"That was some excellent driving, wasn't it?" Kaspar said, glancing proudly at Henrik.

Allissa nodded and smiled weakly.

"Seven-liter engine in this beast," Kaspar said, tapping

the dash. "With Henrik behind the wheel, you'd have to be quick to keep up with us."

They turned a corner and emerged onto a narrow road with an asphalt surface. They bumped up onto the road, turned left and climbed up towards the hill's summit.

"They've got nothing on us," Kaspar said, but not quite so convincingly. He exhaled smoke through the window. "Even if they make it out of there, we'll be done before they've worked out where we're going. That's what it takes to succeed. You've got to do what other people won't. To risk what they can't. Go places they wouldn't expect."

The car slowed for a tight corner and the incline increased. The Mercedes' beams were the only lights within several hundred feet. Henrik shifted gears and they rolled around another sharp bend.

Leo was pleased to see that Henrik's driving had now slowed to a safe and sedate pace. Rather than jarring them forward, the Mercedes now felt luxurious.

"We use this place for our meetings," Kaspar said. "It's not far."

Leo stared into the woodland as they continued to climb. He searched for a glimmer of light or some other indication of where they were going. He couldn't see anything.

Henrik applied the brakes, slowing them to a crawl. A large metal gate materialized from the gloom. Henrik stopped the Mercedes in front of the gate, killed the engine and switched off the lights.

"We're here," Kaspar said, stepping from the car. He pulled one of the bags from the footwell and slung it over his shoulder.

Henrik removed a flashlight from beneath the driver's seat and passed it to Kaspar. Kaspar snapped the light on and walked towards the gate.

Leo and Allissa scrambled from the four by four and followed Kaspar. Leo glanced back at Henrik, waiting in the vehicle. Clearly, he wasn't joining them for whatever was about to take place beyond this gate.

Kaspar removed a heavy chain and padlock from the gate and pulled on the bars. The gate rolled aside on creaking wheels.

"It's all about going to places that others wouldn't think of," Kaspar said, slipping inside.

Leo and Allissa hurried after the German as he paced up the road, the beam of his flashlight whipping from side to side.

Trying to see by the light of Kaspar's flashlight was a challenge, as the beam swept across things, rather than focused on anything. In the sweeping torchlight, Leo saw concrete structures standing all around them.

Kaspar paused and focused the beam of light on a large concrete tower before them. The tower was at least eight stories high and mounted right on the top was a large white dome. Leo saw in the dim light several more domes crowning the other surrounding buildings.

"What is this place?" Leo asked.

"This is Teufelsberg," Kaspar replied, pride lacing his voice. "It means Devil's Mountain. This hill is made from the rubble of buildings destroyed in the war. Because West Berlin was an island inside Soviet territory, they couldn't take it very far, so it was brought here. Millions of tons piled up and covered with earth and trees."

"Look at that," Allissa said, pointing at a mural which was at least fifty feet high. "Who has done all this graffiti?"

Kaspar ignored the question and paced around a dilapidated digger also covered in brightly colored graffiti.

"That's not the interesting part," Kaspar said. "When the

Americans were looking for somewhere to listen to Russian communications, they chose here. No one trusted anyone in those days, all that spying. You see this..." Kaspar angled the powerful torch upwards.

In the milky gloom, Leo and Allissa saw two more white domes high on top of concrete towers.

"Inside these domes they had high-tech listening equipment. They could pick up radio signals from all over," Kaspar said. "This was built as a place of secrets. Now, it makes the perfect place for us too. You know what I mean?"

Kaspar turned on Leo and Allissa with those cold, gray eyes. "We can do what we like on the hill of the devil."

Kaspar turned and paced quickly towards a large metal door. He removed another key and unlocked the door. He pulled the door open, hinges creaking. "This way," he said, stepping inside. His voice echoed from the bare concrete walls.

Leo and Allissa followed. The pair spun from right to left, trying to take in as much of the surrounding building as they could. On the wall beside them, someone's initials appeared beneath a phrase in a language Leo couldn't read.

Leo took a deep breath of damp smelling air. It was a musty odor which seemed to exist as some reminder of the building's past.

Water dripped from somewhere nearby.

They walked through the building for several minutes, following the sweeping beam of Kaspar's flashlight. The place was a maze of rooms and corridors. Some of the spaces had hulking machines and others sat empty. Leo's imagination roamed through the secrets that were once told within the walls.

They reached a staircase and Kaspar started to climb.

Leo and Allissa hurried in pursuit, afraid that getting too far behind would leave them unable to see.

The resonant echo of their footsteps pounded like rain as they climbed. As they rose, Leo tried to estimate how far they were above the ground. Two or three stories right now, perhaps. If they were heading for that main tower, they still had a long way to go.

They continued climbing for what felt like several minutes. Finally, they reached the top of the stairwell and Leo once again felt the night-time air against his face. Kaspar stepped forward and panned his light from side to side.

Leo and Allissa followed, panting hard after the climb.

"Look at that," Allissa said, pointing out at the view. They had climbed the central tower and were now high above the canopy of trees. The various domes and boxy concrete buildings of the station spread beneath them.

Down the hillside, treetops glimmered beneath the pale moonlight, and beyond, central Berlin gleamed like a restless ocean. Leo recognized the red and white needle of the Television Tower at Alexanderplatz.

"Good view, yeah," Kaspar said.

Leo took a tentative step forward and stopped. Leo didn't think the flimsy railing which ran around the side of the tower would offer much protection from a lethal fall.

Then, from the bottomless shadows behind them, came a voice.

30

"Who's this?"

Even though Leo had never heard the voice, he knew instantly who it was. He spun around and saw for the first time, partly obscured by the gloom, but completely recognizable, Minty Rolleston.

"What sort of greeting is that?" Kaspar said, spinning his light towards the voice. "I bring you all this money, and that's how you greet me." Kaspar turned towards Leo and Alissa and shrugged as though the whole thing was a big joke. "That's the problem with helping people. They never really appreciate it. I come up here in the middle of..."

"This is not funny," Minty snapped. "The last time I saw you, we were nearly killed by two men. We had to run across the railway line to escape, remember?"

"That makes sense," Leo muttered, looking at Minty as closely as he could. Although dressed in black, nondescript clothes with a hood pulled up, Leo recognized Minty from the various pictures they'd seen. Minty's beard was unkempt, and his brow furrowed in concern. He looked as though whatever had happened in the last few days had physically aged him.

Minty scowled and shifted his gaze from Kaspar to Leo and then Allissa. "What makes sense?"

"We recovered your phone from the tracks at Warschauer Strasse. That's how we…"

"Kaspar, I'll ask you one more time," Minty barked, whipping back around towards the German. "Who are these people?" Minty sounded out each word individually. Although he was speaking in English, it was clear he was talking only to Kaspar.

"These" — Kaspar replied, mimicking Minty's accent — "are Leo and Allissa. They are a pair of meddling detectives sticking their nose in…"

"What!" Minty exploded, throwing his arms up in disbelief. "And you invited them here to meet me? Why didn't you invite Olezka along too? We could have had a nice little party."

"Ha!" Kaspar grunted out a laugh. "I invited them here because your family sent them here to look for you. They were snooping around asking questions about you today. So, I figured, as everyone is so concerned about you, I'd show them you're okay." Kaspar's voice became deep and angry. "You can stop being so ungrateful."

Minty considered Leo and Allissa for a few seconds. "How do you know they're not working with Olezka?" he said, although his voice now held less conviction than before.

Kaspar laughed, tilting his head, and opening his throat to the sky.

Leo studied Minty's movements. The designer shifted his weight from one foot to the other.

Kaspar leaned forward, his hands on his knees, continuing to laugh.

"Well?" Minty said, frustration growing. "How do you know these people are not working with Olezka? I don't think you realize what's at stake here!"

"How do I know?" Kaspar said, clearly still amused. "You ask me why I know these people are not working with a Russian gangster?"

"Yes?" Minty folded his arms.

"Four very good and reliable reasons," Kaspar said, immediately serious. He held up his fingers to illustrate the point and swung the flashlight around, focusing the beam on Leo. "Number one, look at this guy. No Russian gangster would dress like that. Look at that hair. So untidy. Wouldn't happen. He would be thrown out of Russia before..."

"He's got a good point," Allissa whispered, digging Leo in the ribs with an elbow.

Minty analyzed Leo for a long moment. The fashionista didn't indicate whether he agreed.

Kaspar held up two fingers and continued. "Second, on ne govorit po russki."

Leo and Allissa looked blankly at each other.

Kaspar shrugged and said two more phrases neither detective understood.

"Stop playing games," Minty said after a few seconds of silence. "What does that mean?"

"That means, they don't speak Russian," Kaspar said, finally.

"How do you know? He could be pretending," Minty said, with less conviction still.

"Not possible. You should have heard what we were saying about them in the car." Kaspar spun around and smiled at Leo and Allissa. "It was all nice stuff, I promise. I had to see."

"Number three." Kaspar ignored Minty and held up three fingers. "They know your brother, Charles. He is the one who came to see them and asked them to take the case."

"And fourth?" Minty said, scowling.

"Fourth, and finally, the most compelling reason is..." Kaspar spread his arms like a showman working a crowd. "Olezka tried to follow us here and..."

"He what!" Minty hissed, his tension suddenly returning.

"Relax! Henrik's skillful driving and my quick thinking dealt with that. Put it this way, we won't have any more trouble with Olezka and his men." Kaspar brushed his hands together. "As ever, Kaspar has it all sorted. One step ahead of it all."

Minty frowned.

"You told me you wanted this over with as quickly as possible to stop your family worrying about you," Kaspar said. "I mean, it all sounds strange to me. A few weeks without a phone call and they think you're dead. But who am I to judge?" The German shrugged. "Last time I spoke to my family, I ended up fist fighting with my dad. We smashed up the house good and proper. Mum told me never to go..."

"What's your point?" Minty growled.

Kaspar pointed at Leo and Allissa. "You were worried about your family. These guys can tell your family that you're safe, well, grumpy and ungrateful." Kaspar folded his arms triumphantly.

Minty glared silently at Kaspar for a few seconds, before turning his icy stare on Leo and Allissa. "You're from Brighton?" he asked.

Leo nodded.

"What part?"

Leo thought it was an unusual time to discuss details of their home city.

"What part of Brighton do you live in?" Minty snapped.

"In Hove, two streets back from Brunswick Square." Allissa was the first to reply.

Minty nodded. "And my parents have sent you? I thought they might send someone. This was the reason I didn't want to do it like this." He pointed at Kaspar aggressively. "You told me this would take two days..."

"Hey, I'm not the general manager of the world. Sometimes things take longer than expected. What can be done? Nothing! There were a couple of delays with Olezka not yet out of the picture." Kaspar shrugged as though Olezka was little more than an annoyance.

"By now, I should already be far away from here." Minty pointed vaguely off into the distance. "Still, I have to wait for you, with my family worrying."

"Well, now your family will know you're alright. And you'll have all this money to enjoy." Kaspar held up the bag, rocking it as though tempting a recalcitrant child.

Minty reached for the bag, but Kaspar pulled it away.

"No, no, don't snatch," Kaspar said, playfully.

Minty scowled. "Stop messing around and show me."

"You guys have no, how you say... decorum." Kaspar dropped the bag, squatted beside it, and pulled open the zip. He pushed it across the floor towards Minty. "There you go. All yours, my friend."

Minty knelt, dug a flashlight from his pocket, and snapped it on. He rummaged around inside the bag and removed one bundle of notes. He held the bundle in the beam of light, the notes glimmering. For a few moments, the tension disappeared from Minty's posture, and he gazed excitedly at the cash.

Kaspar turned and faced the outline of Berlin on the horizon.

"It's a shame," Kaspar said, shaking his head. "We could have gone into business together and made this much money every week." He pointed at the bag. "This would have been just the start. The first of..."

"I assume it's all here?" Minty interrupted, tucking the first bundle away and pulling out a second.

"What do you take me for?" Kaspar spun to face Minty. "Of course, it is all there. I am a businessman, not some cheap con-artist." Kaspar poked a finger into his chest. "You do business with Kaspar, and you get..."

"Well, that's it." Minty interrupted again. His movements now hurried, Minty dropped the bundle of notes into the bag and zipped it up. He slung the strap across his shoulder and lifted the bag on to his back.

"Are you sure you don't want to be a part of this business?" Kaspar said, looking out at the city. "It's been good to work with you. Do you want to reconsider? I could make you a very wealthy man."

"No. I never wanted to be part of it. Now I'm getting out." Minty took a step towards the stairs, then froze, and turned to face Leo and Allissa. "Thank you for coming. Please tell my family that I am fine and will be in touch once I'm safely out of the city." He pointed at Kaspar. "Please don't mention to them any of the dealing with him. My mother will have a fit thinking about what I'm involved in."

"My mother will have a fit," Kaspar said, mimicking Minty's accent with surprising success.

Minty turned his gaze to Kaspar. The designer looked as though he were about to shout at the German, then exhaled.

Clearly Minty had now got what he needed and wanted to get out of there with his money. "Whatever you do now, my name stays out of it, okay?"

"Yes, yes, but why the rush all the time?" Kaspar nodded frantically. "Business is as much about the people as it is the money. Don't people realize that anymore…"

"This is not business," Minty hissed. "I never wanted this. I was forced into this by…"

"Oh no, this *is* business." It was Kaspar's turn to interrupt now. The German pointed a finger at the fashion designer. "This has always been business. Business is business. Whether it's fashion or drugs…." Kaspar stepped forward and rested the finger on Minty's chest, "supply and demand my friend, it's all a case of supply and demand."

31

Henrik turned the Mercedes around, reversed up close to the gate and killed the engine. Although with the fire consuming their pursuers' car, the threat should be out of the picture, Henrik didn't want to relax yet.

And, of course, there were still the police to consider. Should they make the link between the destroyed car on the residential street below, and the explosion in the forest, it might lead them this way.

Henrik leaned back in the seat and congratulated himself on a successful day so far. Although there were many things Henrik had yet to learn about the organization, he was pleased that Kaspar had complemented him on his driving.

Henrik checked the rear-view mirror and drummed his fingers on the steering wheel. The domes and towers of the abandoned spy station loomed up behind him. Henrik didn't know why Kaspar insisted on using places like this. Why they couldn't meet in one of Berlin's many parks, he had no idea. It gave him the creeps, coming out into the middle of the forest like this.

Henrik glanced at the clock on the dash. Kaspar had only been gone a few minutes. Henrik glanced down at the bag in the passenger seat footwell. He picked up the bag and unzipped it. Great dirty piles of cash were stacked together, fastened with elastic bands. Henrik removed a bundle and flicked through it. He did some quick calculations and took a sharp inhale. Henrik had never seen so much money. It was exciting to think that if he kept working with Kaspar, that would all change. Money was about to come to them in abundance.

Henrik stashed the money away, pushing it far out of sight, and once again drummed his fingers on the steering wheel. He glanced at the clock. Only two minutes had passed since he'd last checked.

"Come on," he muttered to himself, his stomach churning in a nervous cycle.

Henrik scanned the surrounding forest, reassuring himself that he was here alone. His gaze caught a flicker of movement, something skirting the edge of the forest. He jolted forward in his seat, staring hard. His heart beat an increased tattoo within his chest. For several seconds he stared into the forest, trying to see the moment again. A feeling of unease worked its way up his spine.

Henrik subconsciously pictured the burning car again. Was it possible that Olezka had escaped the inferno and made his way up here, hellbent on revenge?

"Get a grip," Henrik said, forcing a laugh.

As though to prove his own bravery, Henrik swung open the door. The fresh night air streamed in, laced with the hoots and rustles of the forest. The noises brought with them another harbinger of worry. Henrik slid the gun from where it was concealed beneath the seat.

Henrik climbed out of the driver's seat and stalked

forward. He did a full three sixty, his gaze sweeping across the towers of the spy station above him. He saw no sign of Kaspar and the detectives returning yet.

Another scurrying noise reverberated from between the trees. Henrik whipped around towards the sound, bringing the gun up to bear. He stalked towards the tree line, his eyes scanning the gloom for anything that didn't look right.

At the edge of the road, he paused, listening. The woods were deceptively quiet, but Henrik knew better than to trust the silence. The natural stillness of the place was a stark contrast to the urban hum he enjoyed. He drew a small flashlight from his pocket, a beam of light cutting through the surrounding trees.

A rustle to his right drew his attention. Henrik turned sharply, swinging the pistol in line with his sight, as Kaspar had taught him. The beam of his flashlight fell on a pair of yellow eyes, low to the ground. A fox, its coat mottled with shades of red and brown, watched him curiously before darting away into the underbrush.

A wave of relief washed over Henrik as he exhaled a breath, tangled with apprehension. A self-deprecating laugh escaped him, a fleeting respite from the tension.

But that solace shattered in an instant when a sinister voice sliced through the stillness from somewhere behind him.

"If you plan to kill, do it swiftly, without hesitation."

Henrik recognized the guttural, Russian-accented voice in a heartbeat.

"And never get too close," Olezka said.

The soft cough of a silenced pistol punctuated the night, and Henrik's breath caught in his throat. A momentary gasp, a gurgled sigh, and his body crumpled forward onto the cold asphalt.

Olezka's voice was devoid of emotion as he uttered, "There won't be a 'next time' for you." He slipped the weapon under his coat, and then lifted his eyes towards the towers of the spy station.

Olezka gurgled out a laugh. "This place is typical of you, Kaspar. It's fitting that it should be your last." Olezka strode towards the looming structure and was, in a second, swallowed by the night.

32

Minty took a step backward and exhaled. His right arm rested on the bag at his side.

Leo imagined the man's relief. Whatever Minty was involved in, he was clearly glad to be out of it. Leo figured that Minty probably had an escape plan ready. With all that money, he had enough to set himself up somewhere new.

"The offer is there, anyway," Kaspar said, shrugging. "When you've finished 'finding yourself,' and you are once again bored and penniless, you come back to Kaspar, and we will work together. We would have something good going, for sure."

Leo looked from Minty to Kaspar. Although the German continued talking, it was clear that Minty wasn't paying any attention.

Then, sending a chill of ice down Leo's spine, another voice boomed from the darkness. The voice, and the accent, sounded menacing. Although Leo had never met the man, he knew in a heartbeat who it was.

"You thought you could screw us over, did you?"

Leo glanced around in panic. Although the voice came

from close by, the speaker remained cloaked by the gloom. Shapes fanned out from somewhere near the staircase.

"Now you've made me come all this way, to get what's mine."

A figure stepped from the stairs and closed in on Minty and Kaspar.

Leo glanced around. The familiar *thump* of panic now echoing in his ears.

Minty stood frozen to the spot, all color draining from his face. He clutched the bag and held it to his side, his knuckles whitening.

"Olezka," Kaspar said. The sound was more of an inhale than actual words. "I knew I should have walked down that slope and put a bullet between your eyes, just to make sure you were dead.

Kaspar dropped into a position like a sprinter on the blocks, ready to fight or flee. He swung the beam of his flashlight towards the intruder.

When Leo laid eyes on Olezka Ivankov for the first time, he immediately thought that the man resembled a Russian Kingpin in every way. The man was enormous — well over six feet tall — and as wide as a bear. Dressed head to toe in black, Olezka's body rippled with muscle.

Olezka laughed, although to Leo it sounded more like an animal choking on something disgusting. "Kaspar, that is you all over. You are always rushing for glory, never able to see the work through. Too busy dreaming, and not enough action."

Kaspar snarled, and his right hand slipped inside his coat.

"That was a clever trick back there, though, with the four-by-four," Olezka said, pointing a thumb toward the forest. "But, as always, your failure is in underestimating me.

I knew you weren't out here by chance. Once we got out of the car, we followed your tire tracks all the way here."

Leo spun around but couldn't see Allissa. She blended into the shadows that hid the majority of the old spy station. Leo assessed their options and decided that right now they weren't good. As far as he knew, there was one stairwell in the tower, and that was now blocked by Olezka and another man standing a few feet behind.

"Drop that," Olezka barked.

Kaspar's hand, which had been creeping inside the green coat, froze.

A powerful flashlight snapped on from behind Olezka, verifying Leo's suspicion that the big man was not alone.

"Take the gun out, and drop it," Olezka said, taking one slow step towards Kaspar.

Kaspar stood rigid. His eyes panned from right to left. The man was clearly weighing up whether an all-out gun fight was the best course of action.

Leo stared back at Olezka, fear coursing through his veins. Although terrified, Leo was also captivated by what might happen next.

Olezka took another step forward and levelled the gun at Kaspar. The two men were now ten feet away. Without a moment's hesitation, Olezka fired. The silencer made a faint pop of the gunshot. Olezka's muscular arm handled the recoil in practiced efficiency, barely even moving.

The bullet sailed a fraction of an inch past Kaspar's thigh, hit the concrete floor, and ricocheted out into the forest.

Out of instinct, Kaspar clutched his thigh where the bullet almost skimmed his skin.

"If I have to fire again, the bullet will go between your eyes," Olezka said, his voice little more than a whisper. The gun was now levelled at Kaspar's head. "Remove your weapon and push it across the floor now."

Leo stared at Kaspar in silent shock. The scene had an eerie, disconnected quality to it. It was so bizarre that Leo didn't even truly believe it was real. It looked more like one of the gangster films they might watch on a Saturday evening, rather than something that was happening right before his eyes.

Kaspar muttered a few German words. They sounded like swearwords, although Leo couldn't be sure. Finally, Kaspar relented. He fished a gun from beneath the green coat. With a grip on the weapon's barrel, he carefully set it on the concrete.

"Kick it here." Olezka indicated a spot on the floor with his free hand.

Kaspar kicked the gun with the toe of his boot. The gun slid forward a foot and hit an imperfection in the concrete, skipping off to the right. The weapon finally came to a rest three feet in front of Leo.

While Olezka was still concentrating on Kaspar, Leo glanced down at the gun. The weapon wasn't very far away at all but would be useless without a steady and experienced hand to fire it. Leo looked up before Olezka noticed him and considered him to be a threat. Right now, Olezka had barely noticed Leo's presence, let alone considered him to be dangerous. The Russian's lips twisted into the forming of a grin. Olezka was clearly thrilled with the way things were panning out.

33

IN RESPONSE to the sound of the intruder's voice, Allissa acted on instinct. She took three steps backward and ducked in behind a wall. Her timing was flawless, dropping out of sight a second before Olezka's subordinate turned on his flashlight.

The light filled the space, panning right and left before settling on Kaspar and Minty. Allissa, staying low to the ground, crawled to the edge of the wall, and peered around. She hadn't noticed in the dark, but she had crawled behind a small concrete divide which ran halfway across the space.

Olezka stepped from the stairwell and paced towards Kaspar, Minty and Leo. Kaspar clearly recognized the man and leaned forward as though preparing to fight. Allissa didn't fancy Kaspar's chances. The other man was probably twice his size and was armed. Although she knew Kaspar also had a gun, tucked away beneath his coat, it was as good as useless.

Allissa remained riveted to the spot as Kaspar and Olezka exchanged some terse words. Olezka raised the gun and fired his warning shot. Allissa watched as Kaspar's bravado ebbed away. Olezka was a dangerous man with a score to settle.

"Enough of this," Allissa whispered, ducking back out of sight. "We need to get out of here." Although Allissa knew she should feel no loyalty to Kaspar, he was no threat to Minty and Leo. Olezka wouldn't think twice about shooting them all.

Using the wall as cover, Allissa crawled toward the stairwell. Set into the center of the octagonal tower, the stairwell was their only way back down to ground level. The problem was, Olezka currently blocked the only access to the stairs.

When she was out of Olezka's line of sight, Allissa stood up and walked silently around the stairwell. She moved with her fingers running across the wall which enclosed the staircase, both to find her way around, and to check whether the stairs were blocked off on all sides. Unfortunately, the stairs were only accessible from an entrance behind Olezka.

Allissa shuffled around the wall until she had almost completed a total circuit of the tower. Now peering around the last curve, she could see Olezka from the back, with another man standing a few feet behind him.

"How did you think you would get away with stealing from me?" Olezka said, his voice booming through the structure. He was speaking in English, no doubt so that Leo and Minty could understand, too.

"And now you've got these two involved." Olezka pointed at Leo and Minty. The gesture was reassuring to Allissa, as it showed that he hadn't realized that she was nearby. "Whatever happens to them will be in your dirty hands." Olezka swung the gun from Kaspar to Minty and on to Leo. The gesture sent a bolt of fear through Allissa's body. It was confirmation of what she'd expected — Olezka wouldn't leave any loose ends. She steeled her courage and hurried back across the space.

"I'm surprised you thought you could hide away from me," Olezka said, turning to face Minty. Olezka's voice boomed through the ruined buildings. "Whatever you'd done, you were owed a cut of the spoils. I knew you wouldn't go until the exchange. You'd surface soon enough, like a hungry rat."

Using the milky moonlight streaming in through the open sides of the tower, Allissa assessed the scene. She needed to find something that she could use as a weapon. If she could disable Olezka's second in command, that would at least give them a fighting chance. Her heart sank when she saw how empty the building was. Since being deserted several decades ago, everything valuable had already been extracted.

She paced carefully to the edge of the tower and peered out. The ground loomed over one hundred feet below, offering no help whatsoever.

"Ambition, that's your problem," Olezka said, clearly now addressing Kaspar.

"You come here to give me another lecture?" Kasper said, bitterly. "You have wasted so much of my time over the years with your boring—"

"I give you everything," Olezka continued, interrupting his former subordinate. "A great life. More money than you could ever want. The girls. The drugs. And the chance to one day hit the big time. You had it all. But that clearly wasn't enough. You wanted to do it your own way."

"You're stuck in the past, Olezka," Kaspar retorted. "I tried to tell you this many times. The Wall has fallen, and the Cold War is over. You give me no choice but to…"

As the two men slogged verbal punches at each other,

Allissa padded to the other side of the tower and peered over the edge. She noticed that the railing here had come away from the wall.

"That could do," Allissa whispered, gripping hold of the steel. She pulled on the metal bar, working it free from the concrete.

"You know nothing!" Olezka shouted, the sound of his voice conveniently covering the crunching noise the steel made as it finally broke free of the concrete.

Allissa staggered back, surprised by the weight of the heavy bar. She planted her feet shoulder width apart and hefted the bar. In the moonlight she saw it was about three feet long. The thing was certainly strong enough to knock a man unconscious, providing she could get her aim right.

"You think you can stop my supply and give yourself a good payday," Olezka boomed. "You want to get rid of me? Cut the head from the snake, so they say. I might be old, but I'm no fool."

Allissa paced silently back across the tower, using Olezka's voice to home in on the threat.

On the other side of the building, Leo used Olezka's distraction to glance again at Kaspar's gun on the floor. As though tempting him to grab it, the gun had spun and landed with its handle facing Leo. The problem was, Leo had no experience using a firearm of any kind. They had been unfortunate enough to have one pointed at them a few weeks ago.

His eyes returned to the gun again, wondering what sort of safety catch it had. When Leo looked away, he noticed Kaspar throw him a glance, twinned with an almost imperceptible nod.

Olezka continued to rage now, shouting at Kaspar in English, German and Russian. It was impressive how the guy could communicate violently in such a range of languages.

Leo registered Kaspar's nod as a sign that he had to try. With Olezka still distracted, Leo took a half step forward, closing the gap between himself and the weapon. His lack of experience aside, Leo using that weapon was their best chance of survival.

"Enough talking," Olezka said, his stony gaze riveting Kaspar to the spot. "I have a business to run. Fortunately, I have no shortage of good men to help me. Being without one is not a problem. Just another rotten apple." He spun to face Minty, almost turning his back to Leo. "You have my money."

Leo used Olezka's movements to take another step forward. He was now two feet from the weapon.

Kaspar swung round and locked eyes with Leo. "Safety is off," he mouthed, while Olezka was focused on Minty. "Point and shoot." Kaspar turned back to Olezka and scowled, clearly feigning the sort of hopeless anger Olezka would expect.

Olezka clicked his fingers. "Pass me the bag, now."

"No," Minty's fingers clenched around the bag's strap. "I need this money."

Olezka glared at Minty, a smile parting his rubbery lips. Olezka levelled the silenced pistol at Minty's chest. "Whether you live, or die doesn't matter to me." Olezka took a step towards Minty and extended his hand. "In fact, is probably easier if I kill you now."

Minty took a step backward.

Leo used the distraction to take another step towards Kaspar's gun. The weapon was now inches from his toes.

"Don't make this more difficult than it needs to be," Olezka said, in a tone that suggested the pair were sharing a joke. "You give me the money, and we have no problem. My problem is with him." Olezka pointed at Kaspar. "As far as I care, you can go."

"I need this," Minty whispered, taking another step backward. He pulled the bag into his chest like he was protecting a child.

"I'm sure you do," Olezka said. "But I don't care what you need." In one swift movement, Olezka's fingers clenched into a fist and swung into Minty's face. The punch landed with the power of a wrecking ball.

Minty stumbled backward, gasping and yelping in pain. He dropped the bag and took another two steps, almost falling over.

Olezka casually stepped forward and picked up the bag. He swung it to his shoulder.

"That was the right thing to do," Olezka said. "You wanted out, and you might still get out, too. After all, I respect you. You made me lots of money. I haven't shot you yet, so maybe you will get through this."

34

Allissa watched all this from the shadows, pacing as silently as she could towards Olezka's associate.

"Hey, you know, we could keep working together. What you say?" Olezka said, throwing a cunning smile in Minty's direction.

Minty's shoulders slumped with dejection.

"Maybe I'll make you stay and work for me. Maybe money is not worth enough to you. No one is irreplaceable. You have already made yourself look dead, so it's no problem for me to do the job properly."

Allissa took another step forward. The man with the flashlight was three feet away now. From her position, she could now see that this man was armed, too. His gun, however, was pointing into the middle of the group and not at anyone. The man clearly thought that the situation was under control.

Allissa took a moment to size the man up from his silhouette. Although he was only six inches taller than Allissa, he must have been twice her weight. Hand to hand, there would be no contest at all.

"Enough talking," Olezka said, his voice deeper than before. He swung the gun back towards Kaspar. "It's time for me to take out the trash."

Allissa swallowed the ball of nervous energy, which felt like a blockage in her throat. She had one chance to get this right.

Slowly, carefully, she raised the steel bar above her head. She focused on the man's short-cropped hair. She inhaled a deep breath and steadied herself.

"You never should have crossed me," Olezka said, staring hard at Kaspar.

Kaspar leaned forward, his face a mask of pure rage. "You don't have to do this," he wheezed. "I'll go... you'll never..."

"Silence," Olezka barked. "Don't humiliate yourself."

Allissa kept moving until she was right behind the man.

"You know I can't let you go," Olezka said. "Not after what you've done. It is a shame that it must end this way, but you made your choice." Olezka's finger tightened around the trigger.

Allissa locked her gaze on the back of the man's head, where she thought the strike was most likely to knock him out. She raised the bar above her head and swung the rod like a baseball bat.

At that exact moment, disastrously, the man took a step forward.

Allissa's arms tensed, struggling to re-direct the moving weapon. She forced the bar downwards, now aiming for the hand which held the gun. This time she struck a home run. The bar connected with the man's wrist, cracking bone, and sending the gun crashing to the floor.

The man howled in pain and spun around. The flashlight beam whipped towards Allissa, plunging the scene into total darkness. The thug sent a forceful punch in her direction. Allissa ducked. Air whooshed past her ear as the first missed her head by inches.

The thug straightened up and struck again. This time, Allissa blocked the punch with the metal bar. The man whimpered as something inside his fist cracked.

Olezka whirled, momentarily disoriented by the chaos. The Russian tried to take a shot but realized that Allissa was shielded behind his comrade — offering him no clear shot.

Leo leaped into action, his hand clutching the gun and lifting it from the floor. The chill of the metal seared his sweaty palm as he clenched it tightly. He sprung to his feet, the weapon in his hand and his eyes narrowing on the target.

"Aim for the chest and take the shot," Kaspar hissed from a few feet away.

Across the room, Olezka sidestepped, trying to fix his aim on Allissa.

Olezka's associate, focused on the struggle, kicked the flashlight across the floor. The light swung wildly, casting erratic beams that danced across the walls and floor.

Leo focused, trying to get Olezka in his sights. As the lights swept from one side to the other, he swung the gun. His finger tensed on the trigger, ready for the split second that would decide it all.

Olezka's second in command made a grab for Allissa. His fingers grazed her arm, but Allissa twisted away. She swung the bar once more with all her might, and this time it met flesh.

There was a dull thud as the bar struck the man's temple. He cried out, a brief, choked sound, and crumpled to the ground, unconscious.

With his second in command now out of action, Olezka paced towards Allissa.

Leo watched the scene, frozen to the spot. He knew the Russian would not hesitate to fire. Allissa was in grave danger if Leo didn't act now. Leo charged forward, took aim as best he could. He squeezed the trigger.

Several things happened all at once. At first, Olezka fired three times, his silenced gun making a hiss as it discharged. Leo's finger reached the trigger point. As Kaspar had said, the safety was off. A shot howled through the building, the recoil forcing Leo's arms up into the air. He struggled with the gun, only just keeping hold of it.

Ahead, there was a movement in the shadow, but Leo had no idea what was going on.

Allissa saw Olezka closing in on her and leaped for the floor. Three shots zipped above her head and skittered across the concrete. Allissa winced, seriously expecting the next shot to be her last.

The next shot sounded different. It wasn't a hiss like the discharge from Olezka's silenced pistol, but an all-out boom. A deafening blast ruptured the silence, the sound reverberating off the bare walls. The shot pounded throughout the structure. Allissa's ears whined.

Leo recovered from the recoil and took aim again. He wasn't sure what he was aiming at, but anger at the thought of someone hurting Allissa now clouded his vision. He fired again. The gun roared two, three or even four more times — Leo lost count — and then clicked empty. Leo's arms juddered from the shockwave, the echo of the gunshots ringing in his ears. He blinked rapidly, trying to focus as the smell of gunpowder flooded his senses.

35

Allissa remained motionless, breathing heavily. With each shot that howled from somewhere nearby, she expected the crippling pain of a bullet wound. But surprisingly, each report echoed out without the searing pain.

Eventually, the last shot reverberated away, and silence returned to the derelict building. Someone picked up the fallen flashlight, and the beam whipped around the room.

Allissa climbed to her feet, not knowing what she might find.

She turned toward the light. Two men lay motionless on the ground. One had a gash to his forehead. Allissa recognized him as the Russian she had taken down. The second, with two bullet wounds to his chest, was Olezka.

Kaspar, holding the flashlight, marched up to the prone figures and studied each one for a few seconds.

Leo looked blankly down at Olezka. As the realization of what he had done sunk in, he dropped the gun. It banged to the floor.

"That was some great work!" Kaspar said, suddenly full

of energy. "I didn't know you had that in you. Where did you learn to shoot like that? Pow pow!" Kaspar's fingers made the shape of a gun and he pointed at Olezka. Kaspar walked up to Leo and placed a hand on his shoulder. "Serious good work, ja! Maybe I should get you to give that Henrik some classes. When he shoots something, he hits everything but. It's more dangerous for me than the enemy." Kaspar snagged up the gun and tucked it out of sight beneath his coat.

Leo glanced down at his shaking hands. His brain still whirred at a thousand miles an hour as he tried to process what had happened. They were still in potential danger, Leo realized. He shook the thoughts from his mind and looked up at the Allissa. A wave of relief passed over him when he saw she hadn't been injured. The pair, both pale from the ordeal, locked eyes. Leo and Allissa paced instinctively towards one another and merged into a hug.

Kaspar wandered back to Olezka's body and pulled the bag of cash away from him. Olezka's hand remained clenched around the strap at first, as though the Kingpin still didn't want to give away his spoils.

With a grunt of effort, Kaspar pulled the bag away and tossed it towards Minty. "This is yours. Now, let's get out of here."

Allissa and Leo broke off their hug and both exhaled a long and tense breaths. Once again, locking eyes, each realized that the other knew how close they had come to an all-out disaster, but neither was willing to admit it yet.

The howl of a siren cut through the forest from some distance away. Kaspar whipped around towards the noise. "Damn it, someone has called the cops."

"Gunshots have that effect," Leo said, looking toward the

sound. Another siren joined the first, wailing together in a discordant harmony.

"We need to get out of here now," Minty said, the sound jerking him back into focus. He pulled the bag in close to his body. "I'm not risking losing this again. There will be too many questions to answer if the police turn up." Minty glanced down at Olezka and the other man.

"Agreed," Kaspar said, pacing towards the stairs.

No one spoke as they charged down the stairs as quickly as possible. Kasper carried his flashlight at the front, the beam whipping from side to side. Minty followed at the back, lighting the stairs more carefully.

"Whoever you people are, I thank you," Kaspar said as they emerged into the yard at the front of the building. Kaspar closed and locked the door behind them. "At first, I thought you were some meddling detectives. All talk and no action. But that was some serious stuff."

Leo nodded, not feeling good humored enough to respond verbally. He turned back and glanced at Minty, who was walking behind him. The man's face was lined with worry from the harrowing experience.

The sirens wailed again as they hurried down the access road towards the gate. It sounded like they were getting closer now.

The group reached the gate. Leo whipped around one last time and glanced up at the domed towers, looming high into the sky. He supposed that tonight's events were just one more secret to add to the place's nefarious history.

"Henrik, get the car," Kaspar shouted, charging through the gate towards the Mercedes. With the sirens now howling from a few hundred feet away, even Kaspar clearly thought it pertinent to rush.

Kaspar rounded on the driver's door and peered inside. "Henrik, where are you?" Kaspar's voice cut through the forest again, darker this time than before.

Tuning in to Kaspar's worry, Leo and Allissa rushed forward. The driver's seat was empty, and the window rolled down.

"Henrik, stop messing around! We've got to go!" Kaspar's voice was now devoid of all humor.

The sirens rose through the forest again. There were at least two of them, maybe more, all howling in their two-tone cry.

Leo and Allissa fanned out around the Mercedes, both searching the road and the forest beside it. It was Allissa who spotted him first.

"Henrik!" Allissa charged across to the fallen man but knew in a second there was nothing any of them could do. Henrik had two bullet wounds to the chest.

Kaspar rushed across and stared down at his friend for a long moment. His jaw set firm and his muscles tensed as though emotion was physically passing through his body.

The sirens howled again, now joined by the distant growling of engines.

"We need to go," Minty said, sliding into the passenger seat. "Those police cars will be here any moment."

"Minty's right," Allissa said, grasping Kaspar's arm. "There's nothing we can do for him now."

Kaspar muttered a few words Allissa couldn't understand and turned towards the Mercedes. His face remained clenched, and his brows furrowed.

Leo jumped into the driver's seat and started the Mercedes. The engine roared to life and Leo made sure that for now, the lights were off.

Allissa walked Kaspar back towards the Mercedes.

Kaspar paused at the door and peered up at the towers, which looked ghostly in the moonlight. "I will take down your organization one piece at a time," Kaspar growled. "No one will remember your name." He slipped into the back seat alongside Allissa.

Sirens howled from a hundred feet away now and police strobes flickered through the trees.

With everyone inside, Leo threw the Mercedes into gear and stamped on the gas. They pulled off at speed. Leo whizzed around the first corner and saw the blue flickering lights pass in the rear-view mirror.

Leo clenched his teeth. It looked like they were stuck.

"This way," Kaspar said, pointing to a footpath winding its way into the forest on the left. "That's our only chance."

Leo swung the wheel, and they bounced from the road and on to the narrow track.

Twenty feet into the track, Leo watched three squad cars scream past them on their way up to the spy station. The police going in the opposite direction, Leo switched on the lights and sped down the narrow track.

"You'll need to get rid of that gun," Leo said, glancing at Kaspar in the rear-view mirror.

"I will get someone to sort that, don't worry," Kaspar replied. "By sunrise, it'll all be fine. They'll be no trace of you on it at all. It will all be fine..." Kaspar said, his voice not holding the conviction it had a few minutes ago. He slid a hand inside his coat, pulled out his cigarettes and lit up.

No one spoke for two minutes. Leo drove through the forest as quickly as he dared, trying to keep the Mercedes level and avoid some of the larger bumps.

Allissa glanced at Minty, holding the bag tight to his stomach. Although they'd found the man they were looking for, a few things still bothered Allissa. So far, the pieces weren't fitting together as she'd like.

"I owe you my life," Kaspar said, lighting one cigarette from the remains of the next. "Next time you come to Berlin, you are staying with Kaspar. I'll show you the best time of your lives. Just ask for Kaspar. People know who I am."

Leo nodded, although he had no intention of finding out what Kaspar claimed was the best time of your life.

"That way," Kaspar said, directing Leo towards a large path which connected a few minutes later to the gravel track they had traveled up. Eventually, they emerged back on to the residential street.

Leo noticed that the smashed-up car was still on the other side of the road. The car's rear end was crunched in, and windows were shattered.

"Drop me here," Minty said. "It's probably best we don't travel together."

Leo pulled the Mercedes to the side of the road.

Allissa drew out her phone and checked where they were. "We should do the same. Someone might have reported this vehicle for dangerous driving, earlier. It wouldn't take much to tie that together with the bodies at the spy station. The station isn't far from here."

Minty climbed out, his hands never leaving the bag. Leo and Allissa followed.

"I'm keeping this car," Kaspar said, moving to the driver's seat. He pulled the door shut and stared at Minty. "Remember what I said. If you ever want to come back, you know where I am."

Minty shook his head, and without a reply, turned and walked away. Allissa and Leo followed. When they were ten feet away, Leo heard the Mercedes engine growl. He turned and saw Kaspar looking back at him.

Kaspar touched his forehead in something of a salute and then pulled away. As the car picked up speed, Leo saw a thick cloud of white smoke stream out of the window. As the Mercedes sped off, Leo couldn't shake the feeling that he would cross paths with the German again, whether he wanted to or not.

36

"Thank you," Minty said, as the three paced through the quiet residential streets. "I suppose you'll tell everyone what's happened now."

"No," Allissa said, "we don't do this to make headlines. We came here to find you. We will tell your family that you're alive and safe. The rest is up to you."

Minty turned to face the pair. His eyes glistened with emotion.

"I wanted to tell them, but I couldn't risk it. I couldn't even risk the phone call." Minty's stare became unfocused. "If they," — he indicated behind them with a thumb — "caught up with me, there was no telling what they'd do. I wouldn't be here —"

"Whatever you were involved in, it's over now. You're safe," Leo said.

"What problem did those guys have with you?" Allissa asked.

Minty glanced around, as though checking they were alone.

"When I got to Berlin with the vision of establishing an

eco-friendly fashion label, I was way ahead of my era. That sort of thing didn't happen five years ago. Stupidly, I went for it anyway. I sank all the money I could into the shop, setting up the website, sourcing the best ethical materials — all that. But the company needed more and more money."

Leo glanced at a large house with its lights off. Fortunately, it appeared as though the shots from the spy station hadn't been heard this far away.

"The bills mounted up, the rent increased, the cost of production increased," Minty continued. "I was going to have to pack it in. Then I got a visit from Olezka..." Minty's voice dried up and he walked in silence for a few seconds. "Olezka said that he could help me. He seemed to know a lot about the business. He knew my materials were imported from Peru. He knew how often I got deliveries, and he knew I needed the help. He made me a deal. All I had to do was receive some packages. I had to accept them and leave them in the shop for a few weeks. Then, they would be collected. He said he would pay me a thousand euros per package."

"That went on for years. The number of boxes increased, as did the money. For a while it was great. I used some of the money to invest in the business and enjoyed the lifestyle. But it all changed. The men demanded more. They started meeting in the shop, smoking in there, doing deals, taking drugs. I couldn't run a business that way. So, I told them I wanted out. I figured that the business had grown and that I would be alright on my own."

Minty rubbed a hand across his face. Leo wondered whether he had ever told this story before.

"Olezka said that I owed them. He said that he had done a lot for me, and I owed them..."

Minty sniffed and rubbed the back of his right hand with his left. His shoulders slumped.

"Then Kaspar came to me with a proposal. We would keep a fraction of the deliveries hidden for a few weeks. We had the perfect place. It was easy because most of the time the packages were left untouched for weeks, and more arrived every day. They couldn't have been keeping track. When we had enough, Kaspar said he would deal with Olezka and get me out for good. He was going to sell the stock we'd collected, and then we'd split the cash. It was everything I needed. A fresh start."

"You got the money." Leo indicated the bag, which swung from Minty's hand. "What are you going to do now?"

Minty looked at Leo. "We're getting out of here tonight. We've got it all planned. I've been waiting for this." Minty nodded at the bag. "This will get us started, give us long enough to get somewhere safe. We'll see what happens after that."

They turned into another wide, suburban street. Modern and luxurious houses sat within expansive gardens.

"Will you do something for me?" Minty asked, stopping and turning to face Leo and Allissa. "I mean, I know you've done so much already... if you weren't there tonight..."

"Whatever it is, we'll try," Allissa said.

"Let *me* tell my family. I'll call them as soon as we're away from here and safe."

Leo thought of the distraught young man who had met them in their distant Brighton flat two days ago. He knew they should pass on the information straight away. But, then again, a few hours wouldn't make a difference.

"We can wait twenty-four hours," Allissa said, speaking before Leo had decided. "This time tomorrow, we'll call your brother."

Minty exhaled and nodded.

"But it would be better if you told them yourself. You could call them on your way out of the city. You don't even have to tell them where you're going, just that you're okay. That's all they'll want to know."

Minty smiled weakly.

"This is me," Minty said, pointing towards a large house.

"You're staying here?" Leo said.

Minty nodded.

"Good luck," Allissa said, extending a hand. Minty shook it.

"I'm glad we found you," Leo said.

"Thank you, again," Minty said. "I'll contact my family as soon as we're safe." He turned and crossed the road. He stopped and glanced back at Leo and Allissa.

"There's one thing I don't get..." Allissa said, two minutes later as they made their way to the train station. "I get why the guys were after him. I even understand why Minty faked his death. But why *now*? What changed to bring this on?" Allissa stopped and turned. "Wait a minute."

"What?" Leo said, thinking about the police who would already be at the spy station. "We're done here. Let's get back to the hotel and..."

"No, we don't know it all. Quick, follow me." Allissa turned and jogged back towards Minty's house. She ducked in behind the front hedge of the house opposite.

"Are you serious?" Leo followed, grumbling.

"I want to see what happens," Allissa whispered. "Something about this doesn't add up."

"What's that?" Leo crouched beside Allissa and peered through the leaves. "Minty wanted out, and the gangsters said no. It's simple."

"No, it's not, there's more to it," Allissa whispered. "He

said, *we're getting out of here tonight.* There's someone else involved."

Allissa threw Leo a playful glance. Patchy shadows from the surrounding trees patterned across his face.

"Look." Allissa pointed towards the house. A light snapped on inside and a shadow moved from one room into the next.

"Minty admitted that business wasn't going well," Allissa hissed. "He was involved in underhand dealings with the packages, but he said there was no danger. He could deny all knowledge if he wanted."

The shadow in the house disappeared for a few seconds, then another light blazed on the first floor. Two more lights followed.

For five minutes, Leo and Allissa watched for movement. Leo shifted his weight from one foot to the other.

The lights of a car appeared on the driveway and a Volkswagen Golf pulled onto the road and stopped outside the front door. Minty got out and paced to the front door of the house. He pulled the door open, and a rectangle of light flooded into the street. Two suitcases sat on the hallway floor.

Leo and Allissa watched from behind the hedge as Minty carried the first suitcase to the car. He opened the rear door, slid it in and returned for the second. As Minty forced the second suitcase into the already packed car, a figure stepped into the door's rectangle of light.

"I told you," Allissa whispered. "*We're* getting out tonight."

Minty smiled. It was a smile Allissa recognized — the smile a person saves for someone they love.

Minty gave the suitcase a shove, slammed the car door and scampered towards the silhouette.

The silhouette was a woman, Allissa assumed, by the long hair and body shape. Minty whispered something to the woman and kissed her cheek. Taking the woman's arm, Minty led her down the stairs. Watching from behind the bush, it suddenly made sense to Allissa. She understood why Minty needed out, why he needed to leave his life with the Russian gangsters and mysterious packages, why he would risk anything to get away, and why he even felt the pain caused to his family was justifiable.

The woman, who took the steps slowly with Minty's help, was heavily pregnant.

Minty opened the car's front passenger door and helped the woman clamber in. Minty needed a new life. He needed to start again, and he needed to do it properly because he was going to become a dad.

"I told you," Allissa whispered, smiling.

Leo nodded. Allissa was right. The risks involved with mysterious packages from the Russians may have been acceptable for a man on his own, but Minty would have felt differently faced with the prospect of being a father. Children changed things.

"People don't change for no reason," Allissa said.

Minty climbed up to the house for the last time.

"No," Leo agreed. "You're right."

"Circumstances change people," Allissa said. "Sometimes for the bad, but sometimes for good."

As Minty locked the house, Leo grinned. He glanced at Allissa beside him.

Minty posted the keys through the letterbox, then turned. He looked right and left, up and down the street. The habit of someone used to checking over their shoulder perhaps, or someone saying goodbye to a place that had protected him and his family.

Minty wrapped a bright yellow scarf around his shoulders and, with a broad smile, looked directly at Leo and Allissa. With his smile unfaltering, Minty waved. The designer turned to a large plant pot next to the door and removed a camera from amongst the leaves. He had been watching the street the whole time.

"Clever guy," Allissa said as they stood up.

Minty looped the scarf around his shoulders and got in the car. For a moment, the engine's gentle purring was the only sound. The car clunked into gear and pulled away.

Leo stepped out onto the road and raised a hand, too. At the end of the street, the car turned left.

EPILOGUE

One week later. Brighton, England.

"So, let me get this right," Allissa said, walking into the room. Leo sat at his desk, tapping at the computer. "This new client wants us to follow her husband, just to see what he is up to?"

Allissa peered out through the window. The gray-blue patchwork of the sky looked cold. Leo had wedged the ancient sash window open with a guidebook, and fresh, salty air streamed in.

"That's it." Leo spun on the chair to face her. "It sounds simple, doesn't it? I know we rarely take this sort of jealous marital stuff, but this one seemed too good to refuse."

"What's the difference here? We've turned down loads of cases like this. The missing partner has usually left because the relationship is over."

"I know, I know," Leo said, offering a *don't shoot the messenger* hands up gesture. "And I know what you say. Those people don't need our services. They need to see a therapist."

"Exactly." Allissa placed her hands on her hips. "So, what's the difference here?"

Leo spun to his computer and pointed at a map on the screen. "She knows where he is, and that's a tropical Caribbean Island."

Allissa glanced out at the gray clouds and shivered. "Okay, you've got my attention. But why does she need us if she knows where he is? We find *missing* people. There's a subtle clue about that in our company name."

"That was my question at first," Leo said, clicking through to a different web browser. "The client mentioned that she would be happy to fly us to the island, and book us into a five-star hotel down the road from where her husband is." Leo pointed at the pictures of sandy beaches and blue water that now filled the screen.

"But what do we have to do?" Allissa leaned forward and looked hard at the screen. "There's no such thing as free, after all."

"And nothing is ever as simple as it first seems," Leo added. "The client is specific about this. All we need to do is monitor who comes and goes from his house. She hasn't even said why."

"She must think he's up to something," Allissa injected.

"Clearly, maybe he is. Maybe he isn't. Do you care if we get to spend a few weeks on the beach?" Leo glanced up at Allissa.

"Wait a second," Allissa said. "If we're sitting in some mosquito-infested bush outside this guy's house all day, that's hardly relaxing. Think about all the creepy crawlies that'll be in there."

"Well, we would have to do it like that." Leo clicked to another internet browser. "If I hadn't ordered this."

Allissa leaned again. On the screen was a battery-powered remote-control camera system that could operate from up to a mile away. With the included stake, the system could be concealed in flower beds, bushes, or pots effortlessly.

"Didn't we see..." Allissa said.

"Yep, Minty had one outside his house. That's how he knew we were spying on him. It got me thinking how useful something like that could be, and then this lady contacted us..."

"Is it legal?"

"I... I don't know." Leo spun back to the computer screen. "It doesn't say. But do you really care? We'll set this up near the guy's house, and we can watch the lot from beside the pool."

"I see." Allissa straightened up, beaming. "Now we're talking. When do we leave?"

"I'll just get..."

The door entry system buzzed, interrupting Leo.

"Oh, that thing's working." Allissa turned towards the door where the handset and screen were mounted on the wall. She picked up the phone and looked at the screen. Black and white lines flickered, but no picture materialized. A distorted, incomprehensible voice cracked from the speaker.

"I'll come down," she said into the handset before replacing it on the cradle. "Nope, that's still broken."

With their company being registered to the flat, they got multiple deliveries every day. The problem was the intercom didn't work. That meant delivery drivers assumed no one was in and took the parcel to the sorting office, which was nearly two miles away. Thinking about the annoying journey to the sorting office, Allissa rushed down the twisting stairs. Turning onto the final staircase, Allissa saw an outline through the glass door.

"I'm coming, one minute!" she shouted.

Stepping over piles of junk mail and darting around an old bike which always seemed to be in the way, Allissa threw open the door.

"Hi," she said, out of breath. The gasping reminded her she really should get into an exercise routine soon. "Sorry it took so long. The system's broken and we're on the top floor."

"Parcel for Leo Keane." A delivery man held out a box.

"Yeah, sure, I'll take that." Allissa took the package, scrawled her signature, and climbed the stairs.

"I've e-mailed to say we'll do it," Leo shouted as Allissa let the door slam behind her. "She's going to send the deposit for the flights and hotel today. It could be a nice little earner."

"Cool." Allissa crossed the room and placed the package on his desk. "We best get ready. We're not going to miss Lucy's party again this time."

"Are you sure you want me to come?"

"Absolutely," Allissa said. "Lucy rearranged it especially so that you could join us. She said it was a special sort of thing."

Leo rolled his eyes.

"Before you say anything; I do not know what it's going to be like, and yes I really want you to come," Allissa said.

"Okay," Leo said, knowing he was beaten. He picked up the package. "What's this?"

"It's something for you. I bought it for the party. I think you'll like it." Allissa tried, but spectacularly failed to hide her grin.

Leo glanced nervously at her and pulled the strip seal

from the packet. He looked inside. His forehead creased with confusion, before turning into frustration. "Oh no, no way. It's not happening. You can take this back right now!"

"A deal is a deal," Allissa said, howling with laughter.

"Yeah, but I didn't think..." Leo tipped up the parcel and a bright purple shirt slipped out on to the desk. "Wait a second. How did you even get this?"

"You were in luck," Allissa said grinning. "Minty's brother had one in your size. He'd hardly worn it too. Just think how much Minty was selling them for on his website."

"Minty was selling them for that price because his business was a front for—"

"Oh, shush." Allissa placed a finger across Leo's lips. "A bet is a bet. We found Minty in less than two days. That was the deal."

"That wasn't a bet! That was a..." Leo folded his arms, his mind searching for a way to wriggle out of his promise. "It was a passing comment, you know?"

"Nope. That isn't how I remember it. You made the deal." Allissa pointed at Leo and then dramatically checked the time. "Hurry, the taxi will be here in twenty minutes. Go and put your new purple shirt on."

As Leo grabbed the shirt and stormed out of the room, Allissa laughed out loud. Things had worked out better than she'd expected.

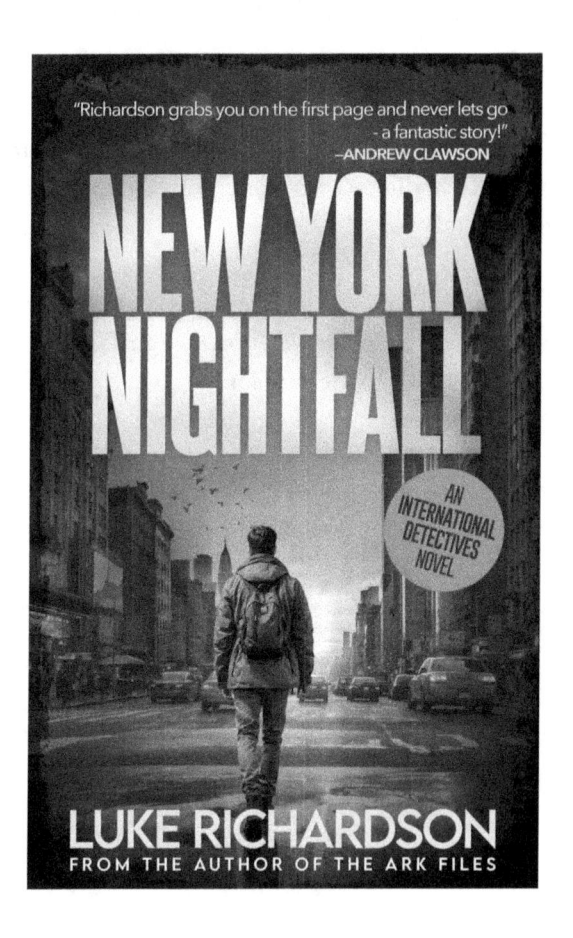

A serial killer stalks the streets. The city lives in fear. The winter of terror is here.

Andy and Emma head to New York, hoping a holiday will repair their strained relationship. When Andy disappears without a trace, it's clear the city that never sleeps has other plans.

Teaming up with New York P.I. Niki Zadid, Leo and Allissa take the case. But, when a mutilated body turns up, and their investigation entangles with the plans of an unhinged killer, a difficult search turns deadly.

Can Leo, Allissa and Niki find their man without falling foul of the murderer's sickening endgame?

New York Nightfall is Luke Richardson's fifth fiery international thriller. Grab your copy to continue this series today!

Search your local Amazon store, your favourite bookseller, or ask in your library for **New York Nightfall by Luke Richardson.**
www.lukerichardsonauthor.com/newyork

A dream proposal turns into a heart-stopping nightmare when Leo's fiancée vanishes without a trace in the tropical paradise of Koh Tao.

Travelling the world with the love of his life, Leo's looking for the perfect place to propose. Reaching the Thai tropical paradise of Koh Tao, he thinks he's found it.

But before he gets an answer, she's nowhere to be seen.

On searching the resort, his tranquillity turns to turmoil. What began as a dream escape swiftly spirals into a harrowing quest as he must to work out whether this is a practical joke gone wrong, or something much more sinister.

Discover where it all began in KOH TAO BETRAYAL, the compelling introduction to Luke Richardson's Best-selling International Detective Series.

Grab your FREE copy now!
www.lukerichardsonauthor.com/kohtao

AUTHOR'S NOTE

Music has been a big part of my life for a long as I can remember, and this is the first one of my novels to include it. I loved writing the various nightclub scenes here. The DJs mentioned are friends of mine too—although they may be so underground that even Google doesn't know about them (yet). As such, I dedicate this book to everyone I've danced with. Whilst there are way too many of you to mention by name, and I am bound to offend by trying, know that the moments we've spent getting lost in the music are very special to me.

I do want to make a special mention, though, to those who are now dancing, singing and partying elsewhere:

Peter Clough
Craig "Chopper" Hutchinson
and Paul Revill
To quote the 1998 hit by house music trio Stardust, *"the music sounds better with you."*

For reasons I can't wholly understand, Berlin is one of my favorite European cities. Maybe it's the music, which you can't help but hear pounding from the open windows of bars, nightclubs or people sitting in the parks. Maybe it's the intrigue of its checkered history, which is still plain to see when walking around the city. Or maybe it's just the fact that over the years I've spend several wonderful weeks there with friends and Mrs. R.

One of the most intriguing sites in Berlin (or rather, just outside Berlin) is the abandoned spy station where the climax to this story takes place. The station is exactly as described here, with its tattered radar domes still visible for miles around. The structure sits on top of the man-made hill called *Teufelsberg* – Devil's Mountain. This man-made mound, built from the city's World War II rubble, conceals beneath it an unfinished Nazi military college.

During the Cold War, though, it became a listening station—a hub of espionage where American and British intelligence operatives eavesdropped on Soviet and East Bloc communications. It's haunting to think about the secrets that would have passed through those corridors and how it may have played a part in the Cold War.

I actually tried to visit Teufelsberg twice before being successful. On my first two visits the site was closed, and with triple fences topped with barbed wire, I wasn't going to attempt a break in.

On the third time of trying, long after this book was first published, I made the walk again to find the station open. It's now become something of an alternative tourist hot spot, with a bar and incredible graffiti. Definitely worth a look if you're in the city!

The nightclub featured here is also like many I visited during my visits. As a lover of electronic music, the nightclubs of Berlin are unparalleled. The scene has a rich and fascinating history that dates back to the early 20th century. In the 1920s, during the Weimar Republic, Berlin was known for its thriving cabaret culture and vibrant nightlife. Clubs like the Eldorado and the Moka Efti were famous for their flamboyant performances and diverse clientele, including artists, intellectuals, and members of the LGBTQ+ community.

After World War II and the division of Berlin, the city's nightlife scene evolved differently in the East and West. In West Berlin, clubs like the Dschungel and the Risiko emerged as key venues for punk and new wave music in the 1970s and 80s. These clubs played a significant role in shaping Berlin's alternative culture and political activism.

In East Berlin, nightlife was more restricted and controlled by the state. However, in the 1980s, illegal parties and underground clubs began to emerge, providing a space for East Berlin's youth to escape the confines of the authoritarian regime.

After the fall of the Berlin Wall in 1989, the city's nightlife scene underwent a dramatic transformation. Abandoned buildings and factories in the former East Berlin were converted into makeshift clubs, giving rise to a new era of techno and electronic music. Clubs like Tresor, E-Werk, and Bunker became legendary for their marathon parties and cutting-edge music.

Today, Berlin is widely regarded as one of the world's premier nightlife destinations, with a diverse array of clubs catering to different tastes and subcultures. The city's clubbing scene is known for its open-mindedness, creativity, and inclusivity, attracting visitors from all over the globe.

During the years I was a school teacher, it was my dream to go and stay in a place and write a book about it while I was there. This book marks a part completion of that dream as while re-writing this book in 2023, Mrs. R and I spent a week in Berlin. As such, this is one of my favorite rewrites of the series.

During that re-writing process, I realized several shortcomings in the first version, including a lack of Berliners in the story. This is especially important because the people of Berlin—be them locals who have lived in the city their whole lives, the creatives who flock there for Berlin's artistic merits, or those who have ended up there for any other reason, make the city what it is.

Once again, although the words here are my own, the characters, experiences and some of the events described are wholly inspired by the people I've traveled beside.

If we ever shared noodles from a street-food vendor, visited a temple together, played cards on a creaking overnight train, or had a beer in a back-street restaurant, you are forever in this book, and for that, I thank you!

Again, thank you for coming on the adventure with me. I hope to see you again.

Luke

THE ARK FILES

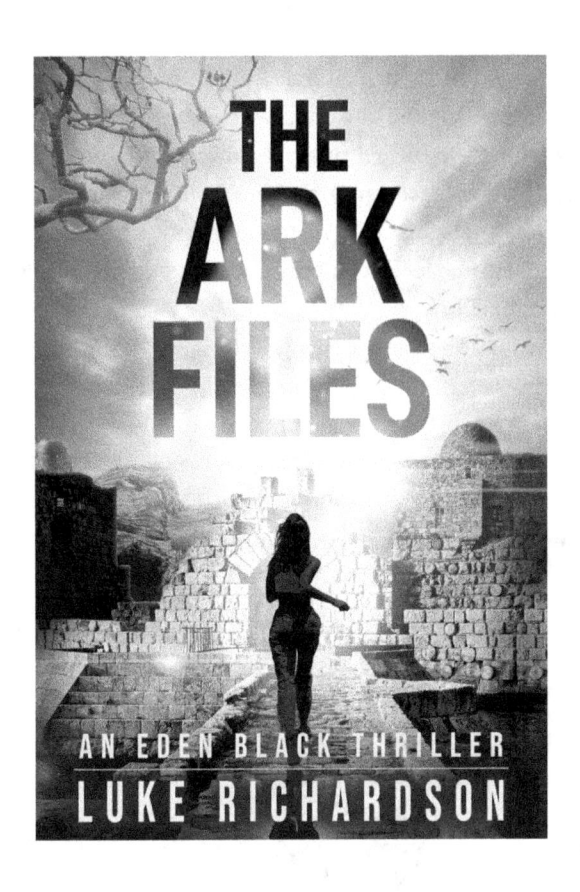

AN EDEN BLACK THRILLER
LUKE RICHARDSON

A secret society...
An ancient manuscript...
One woman to save the world...

Professional treasure hunter EDEN BLACK is no stranger to action. After all, the artifacts she spends her life returning to their rightful owners aren't always easy to access.

When Eden's father dies in a plane crash, her life's turned upside down. Grief turns to fear when she learns that it wasn't an accident. Everyone involved in an archaeological dig twenty years ago has met with a similar untimely end. Everyone that is, but Eden who was ten at the time.

When her father's house is raided and burned to the ground, Eden's forced into action. To learn the truth about her father's death and save herself from sharing his fate, Eden must uncover the manuscript and expose its secrets once and for all.

But this time the world is watching, and not everyone is on her side.

THE ARK FILES is the first in a brand-new pulse-pounding archaeological thriller series by Luke Richardson. Fans of Dan Brown, Clive Cussler, and Ernest Dempsey will devour this in hours!

www.lukerichardsonauthor.com/arkfiles

Or search your local Amazon store, your favourite bookseller, or ask in your local library for **The Ark Files by Luke Richardson.**